# Sour PICKLE

by JJ Knight

# Salty PICKLE

**by JJ Knight**
the *USA Today* bestselling author of

Big Pickle ~ Hot Pickle ~ Spicy Pickle
Tasty Mango ~ Tasty Pickle ~ Tasty Cherry
Royal Pickle ~ Royal Rebel ~ Royal Escape
Juicy Pickle ~ Salty Pickle ~ Second Chance Santa
The Wedding Confession ~ The Wedding Shake-up
Not Exactly a Small-Town Romance
Single Dad on Top ~ The Accidental Harem
Uncaged Love ~ Fight for Her ~ Reckless Attraction

Want to make sure you don't miss a release?
Sign up for emails or texts at www.jjknight.com/news

Edition 1.0

Casey Shay Press
PO Box 160116
Austin, TX 78716
www.jjknight.com

**Paperback ISBN: 9781938150258**

## ABOUT SALTY PICKLE

**I'm headed to New York for the first time. With my goat. I'm eight months pregnant.**

Oh, and I'm barefoot. (The goat eats shoes when she's nervous, and we're definitely wild balls of anxiety.)

The man I'm meeting in his big fancy New York office is the saltiest hunk of male beauty you never want to cross. He wouldn't know a smile if you drew one on his face.

I slept with him on a dare on New Year's Eve. Eight months ago. Eight months pregnant. Yeah, you get it now.

I was going to raise the baby in my Colorado yurt with my pet goat Matilda. My two best girlfriends were going to be the other moms, but their lives moved on.

I'm a yoga teacher with forty dollars to my name.

So I'm loading Matilda onto the subway and headed to Wall Street.

It's time to confront a salty baby daddy in a place called Pickle Media.

# 1

## LUCY

My sweet baby girl Matilda is not impressed by the New York subway.

The press of bodies is like slow dancing with a hundred sweaty strangers, except nobody is having a good time.

It reminds me of my first middle school dance. Too many people. Too much angst. Everybody felt like they had to be there but would have preferred sitting on the sofa, binge-watching Netflix.

And yet, here we are, swaying to the music of the screech of metal.

I look down at Matilda. Her steely blue eyes meet mine. "We're not in Colorado anymore," I tell her.

The lights flicker as we approach a station, like the car is about to blink into the *Twilight Zone*. When the doors open, I push against the tide of exiting passengers and snag a seat, pulling Matilda with me.

The open space in front of us is a temporary relief.

A squeal in the machinery below startles Matilda, and she backs even closer against me.

As the subway car fills up again, we both shrink away from the crush of strangers. We're weary of the unnatural smell of engine oil and too many people.

It's the total opposite of our yurt in the mountains.

"You're okay," I tell her, shifting my knees so she can move closer to the bench.

She's my best girl.

My everything.

I'm so glad I moved heaven and earth to keep her with me on this journey.

But then, a shopping bag smacks into her precious little face.

She turns her long fuzzy nose to me and lets out a plaintive *meh-eh-eh-eh.*

Oh, right. I should have said that up front.

I'm traveling through New York City with a two-year-old, snow-white Nigerian dwarf goat.

And she needs to be milked.

I try to move Matilda out of range of a man in a black suit with an open collar, tightly fitted pants, and baby-smooth *mankles* showing over shiny shoes. How can he walk in those? I wear socks with my Birkenstocks, and they're already comfortable and worn. Those must be killing him.

He hasn't noticed how his Gucci bag keeps knocking into Matilda. The corner pokes her forehead.

She lets out another unhappy bleat. Several people look our way. I give them a big everything-is-just-fine, nothing-to-see-here smile.

I tuck her tightly between my knees. "Shhh, Matilda."

This has been the hardest part of the journey. We boarded at a subway station in Queens, fresh off the feed truck I'd hitchhiked on. I didn't have a lot of options, coming from Colorado with a goat.

But there was no way I would leave my baby behind. Besides, my two best friends had already deserted me. I didn't have a goat-sitter.

It's just me and Matilda with them gone. I've even lost my friendly yoga students after I had to quit teaching class due to the strain on my belly. The doctor made me put a pause on exercise.

Yoga and goat milk are the basis of my entire income, keeping me in herbal tea and tofu, and Matilda in fresh feed and the occasional carrot. But with yoga out for the foreseeable future, I'm stuck. Goat cheese doesn't pay the bills.

And thus, I've come to Manhattan with a knapsack stuffed with feed and forty dollars to my name. I've gotten by so far on luck and kindness, but there seems to be a lot less of it now that I'm in the city.

The subway car screeches to a stop, forcing me to clutch Matilda to avoid tilting into our neighbors. Nobody else seems to notice the shift in movement. They're probably used to traveling like cattle.

A wavering voice next to me says, "You know, you're supposed to keep pets in a carrier."

I turn to the woman. She has sleek gray hair and huge red glasses. Her checked suit and shoes undoubtedly cost more than my yearly income.

Tucked in her lap is a supple red purse with a furry face sticking out. A Pomeranian, by my guess, although it's groomed within an inch of its life.

"I don't think Matilda would appreciate being in a bag," I say.

"Hummph." Her disapproving lips pinch together like a squished tomato.

Will she tell on me? Nobody stopped me from getting on the subway with a goat. Of course, I hadn't seen a single attendant or official-looking person in the station. We'd followed a lady with a baby stroller through a pair of swinging gates, then got on the first train going to Manhattan.

As the subway moves forward, an older gentleman sits next to me. "I used to have a goat," he says and reaches down to pet Matilda.

She preens under his hand like a puppy. She's full grown but barely tops the knees of most travelers. Her beautiful white coat is broken only by the cotton diaper tied to her hindquarters. Pooping on the subway would definitely get us kicked off.

I beam at my new neighbor. I knew I'd find my people here. "What was your goat's name?"

He sits back in his seat. "Oh, we didn't name them. They were meat goats. Raised them until their fat, round bodies were ready for the butcher. Made the best stew."

I can't stifle my gasp, pulling Matilda away from him.

He sniffs. "Don't worry. I see she's a milk goat. She a good producer?"

As if my baby is nothing more than a factory!

Except... she *is* a good producer. I can't help but be proud of her and say, "Two quarts a day."

"Nice. I do love a hearty goat cheese."

I glance down at her. Oh, no. Matilda's nosing her way into a mother's diaper bag, probably foraging for snacks. I try to pull her back, but then one of the lightning-quick pains rockets across my midsection. I suck in a hard breath and press my hand to my belly.

The woman next to me leans away. "You're not in labor, are you?"

Right. I forgot to mention that, too. I'm eight months pregnant. I'm headed to meet the father.

I didn't call. I don't have a cell phone.

I didn't email. No computer.

He has no idea. I'm going in cold and hoping for the best.

But first, to breathe through this pain.

The man next to me sounds alarmed. "Should we call an ambulance? Are you due?"

My voice is a squeak from the darting cramps. "No. I have a month to go. It's just pregnancy pains."

The woman frowns like she doesn't believe me, sure I'll shoot a newborn out onto her red leather pumps.

"Does the baby's father work in the financial district?" the man asks. "He should have gotten you a car."

"I think so," I say.

"You don't know?" The woman's tomato lips tighten again.

The pain finally eases, and I can talk normally. "I only knew him ninety minutes." *Give or take.*

"Ninety minutes!" Both the lady and the man cry the words at the same time. This makes even more passengers turn their heads to look.

I lower my voice. "I mean, it only takes five, right?" I plaster on the same smile I did at my yoga studio when the questions came about my growing belly.

Of course, at that point, April and Summer were planning to be the other two moms. We would raise the baby in love and sunshine and unbridled femininity. Make flower crowns from the meadow. Swim naked in the rivers.

But April got a chef internship in France.

Then Summer met a guy and eloped to Vegas, of all the horrible places, full of unnecessary electricity and poor decisions.

And that left me and Matilda to raise the baby.

The man shifts next to me, probably uncomfortable with my situation, or my defamation of male performance, or both. Whatever. I don't care what he thinks.

I shouldn't, right? Sometimes a girl gets in a situation.

But this guy was something. Tall. Gorgeous. I wasn't looking for a future.

I got one, though.

The woman tugs out a handkerchief and waves it as if I have bad juju she should ward off. Or maybe Matilda is pooping in her wrap. "Are you headed to the financial district? In the middle of the workday? With that *thing*?"

Here we go again. "Matilda is not a thing."

"Now now," the man says. "Don't be mean to the girl. She's obviously in a real pickle."

Funny he should say that. Pickle Media is the name of the company I found when I looked up the man I got dared into flirting with eight months ago.

I check Matilda's diaper wrap. Yep. Poop. Great. Now she needs both milking and a clean-up.

The woman stands as the car slows, tucking her dog under her arm. "Thank God this is my stop."

The man chuckles and pulls himself up by the silver pole. Apparently, it's his stop, too. "Good luck. If you start selling goat cheese in the city, look me up. Stanley's Emporium."

"You're Stanley?"

"The one and only." He laughs. "Among the Stanleys in New York." The door opens, and he moves toward it.

I study the map on the wall and count the stops until I'm in range of Wall Street. Six. I feel a tickle on my feet and look down to see Matilda chewing on the strap of my shoe.

"No, no, baby." She nibbles when she's nervous. I tuck my feet under the bench, but she's eaten halfway through the strap. I'll fix it later.

The car lurches forward. I tighten my gut as much as I can with an eight-month pregnant belly to avoid tilting into the teen girl who has plopped down next to me.

I guess I do stick out here in my socks and sandals, the elastic of my colorful paisley skirt pulled up over my belly so it'll fit, and my choppy self-cut hair. But there's nothing I can do about it.

I'm having a baby in a month. April and Summer are gone, along with their car and cell phone. My job at the yoga center is on hiatus, with no more access to running water and a bathroom since I handed in my key to the building.

I'm at my last resort.

And believe me, if Court Armstrong is even close to as brooding and salty as I remember, he's absolutely *the last resort*.

## 2

## COURT

L iterally nobody at Pickle Media likes their job.

I stare at the summary of this quarter's performance reviews and wonder how the hell I'm going to forward them to Uncle Sherman.

After last quarter's fell dramatically, I assumed something was wrong with the supervisors conducting the reviews and hired an outside firm.

But this impartial third-party company found things were even worse.

I scan some of the phrases taken from the employees.

*Crappy work culture.*

*Nobody wants to be here.*

*Only the pay is worth it.*

Then the conclusions of the reviewers.

*Low work morale.*

*Little opportunity to showcase their skills.*

*Planning to move on whenever possible.*

I spin away from the monitor. This is on me. Pickle

Media was fine when I took it over from the people Uncle Sherman hired to establish it, while I was getting my master's degree in business.

What can I do to change something that's clearly poisoned all the way down to the administrative assistants?

I clasp my hands behind my head. This day sucks. Maybe I'll take the rest of it off. Hit the gym. Get too exhausted to think.

I pick up my cell phone. I could reinstall Tinder, do some swiping.

I haven't done that in nearly a year. It hasn't appealed.

Nothing does.

My assistant texts me. *There's a woman to see you.*

Now what? Devin never says, "A woman." He gets their name and credentials. And since when does someone get to pop in to see the CEO without an appointment?

I pick up the desk phone and hit the button to buzz him.

Devin picks up. "I was trying to be discreet."

"What the hell for?"

"It's a… situation." His voice is low. Devin's voice is never low.

I hang up, realizing a second too late I should probably have been polite about it. I text him back.

*Me: Who is she?*

*Devin: She won't say.*

*Me: I'm sure it's some useless sales pitch. Send her to Beth.*

*Devin: I don't think so. She has a goat.*

I stare at the words a moment. A goat?

Then a curdle of unease spreads in my stomach. I met a woman with a goat once. I was at the Castle Hotel in Colorado, near my family's house. It's indirectly in the Pickle empire, since the owner is the sister of my cousin's wife.

As Uncle Sherman likes to say, *every Pickle's a Pickle.*

The Castle staff let the woman keep the goat in the stables with the Avalonian donkeys they raise.

What was her name?

Linda?

Loretta?

No, it was cuter.

Lucy. That's it. Lucy… something.

*Me: Ask her if her name is Lucy.*

I wait, wondering why she's here. I met her in the hotel bar, a funny cantina with a haunted theme. She'd been pushed toward me by two of her friends.

I ended up in her room for an hour or two. Yeah, we did shit. All consensual. Condoms in accordance with the laws of first-name hookups.

Now she's in New York?

Devin finally replies, *Yes. She seems relieved you remember.*

I guess I'll see her. *Send her in.*

The smell hits before the door is fully open.

Livestock. Earth.

The goat comes in first, looking around like he owns the place. Or, maybe it's a she. I think Lucy mentioned her goat's milk supply. Now that's pillow talk.

But when Lucy enters, belly first, I jump out of my chair.

She's pregnant. Like, really pregnant. Her colorful skirt covers a huge ball of belly. How many months ago were we together? It was New Year's Eve, and now it's August.

Eight months.

Is that eight months pregnant?

My gut tightens. This has to be why she's here. Did she smell money and decide to pawn the kid on me?

Not without DNA testing.

But what if it is mine?

I'm hosed.

Thoroughly hosed.

Lucy walks into my office with an uncertain smile. She tucks her golden-brown hair behind one ear.

Her feet are… bare.

Is she really showing up here barefoot and pregnant? With a goat?

"Hello, Court," she says.

I can't find my voice for a second. She's mostly as I remember—pretty and friendly, with farm-girl vibes.

But that belly.

I gesture to a chair and clear my throat. "Hello, Lucy. Sit down, of course. Is the goat okay?"

The animal nibbles at the leather padding on the chair next to her.

"Matilda, no! Don't chew the furniture." Lucy pulls the goat close. "She's nervous. She already ate through the strap of my shoes." She lifts a foot and wiggles her toes.

That solves that mystery. Now for the bigger one, why she's here.

I sit, glad the imposing desk is between us. "Can I help you?"

"I... uh." She falters, looking around the room. "This office is nice. I saw you're the CEO. You didn't tell me that."

I specifically left out work details the night we met. "How did you find me?"

"You said you worked in New York. The bartender already told us that you were part of the Pickle family. Turns out Court and Pickle together aren't that common as names. I mean, once you knock out pickle-ball, the sport. It led me to your staff picture. I knew it was you."

"You couldn't call?"

She shuffles her feet on the rug. The goat has resumed chomping at the leather of the chair.

"I don't have a cell phone. At least, not anymore. Not when I decided to come. My friend April—you might remember her, the one with red hair—she had the phone. But she's gone to France."

And Lucy has no access to one? No email? A growl forms in my throat, ready to accuse her of all sorts of things. Extortion. Playing on my sympathy, like I have any left.

"So you thought it was better to simply show up unannounced? I assume you drove, given the goat?"

Her fingers twiddle with a fold in her colorful skirt. "I, uh, don't have a car either. Summer drove us to the Castle that weekend we met. She took off in June to Vegas with some guy named Tommy. They got married."

"So you flew? They let the goat on the flight?" They really were getting permissive on the airlines.

"No. I rode here on a feed truck. A nice man from Ohio. That was after a trucker got me halfway here."

I almost stand from the shock but force myself to remain planted in my chair. "You hitchhiked from Colorado?"

"It's not hard. The goat helps. I mean, not for regular people in normal cars. They don't want you messing up their seats. But delivery people. They like company."

"Anything could have happened! And you're pregnant!"

She shrugs. "It makes men less likely to get handsy. They're squeamish."

They shouldn't be. She's rosy and glowing, and I'm already flashing with everything that happened in that encounter between us in Colorado.

Time to address the elephant in her belly. "Is that why you're here? The pregnancy?"

She notices the goat gnawing on the chair. "Oh, no!" She pulls her away. "I'll pay for the damage. Somehow. Oh. Gosh. Oh." Then the waterworks start.

Bloody fucking hell. She's going to cry on me. Of course she is. "Don't worry about it. I'll have maintenance take it to be fixed."

She pulls a few stalks of hay from her knapsack and holds it out, tears streaming down her cheeks. "She's been short on foraging since we got to Queens. The subway ride was hard on her."

"You took the subway with a goat?"

"How else would I get here?"

This whole thing is ridiculous. Who does this? It's an episode of a TV comedy. Or a bit in a stand-up routine.

"About the pregnancy," I remind her. "Is it your assertion that the child is mine?"

She focuses on the goat chewing through the hay. "It *is* yours. There was nobody before you, not for months. And nobody after."

"I'm supposed to believe you?"

Her head snaps up at that. "Of course you are. You were there."

"Properly sheathed in a condom."

"With eighty percent effectiveness."

"When used improperly, which wasn't the case."

She swipes away her tears. She's switched to angry. I can see it in her steely posture, the uplift of her chin. "It could have been defective."

"Why aren't you on birth control?"

She lets out a huff. "Why would I put unnatural hormones into my body?"

Oh, now I'm remembering. She's a yoga, vegetarian, crunchy-granola naturalist. Eight months ago, she'd gone on quite a while about the ills of modern industrial society.

Not that she's wrong. But she takes it to an impractical level. In fact, I think she lives off the grid.

Which explains the no phone, no email, no car.

"When can we do a DNA test?" I ask her.

Her face pales, two bright spots of pink standing out on her cheeks. "I have no idea."

"You hitchhiked here all the way from Colorado,

and you don't even have a way to prove that this pregnancy is mine?"

Then it happens again. The waterworks. She sniffs. She wipes her eyes.

Holy Christ. I don't know what to do with this.

She points at my computer. "Can you look it up?"

"Look what up?"

"DNA tests."

I'm happy to spin away and face my monitor. The impassive glow of technology is vastly preferable to her misery.

She sniffles while I tap and scan the results.

I speed-read the first hits. "You can do it while pregnant, but it's an invasive procedure."

"A needle? Like amniocentesis?"

"Yes."

She makes a little cry.

"But once the baby is out, it's a simple swab of saliva."

Another cry.

I want to read more than headlines about how this works, but I turn back to her. I try to imagine what a kinder, gentler person would do. Someone like, I don't know, my brother Axel. Or my cousin Anthony. Maybe all the patience went to the A names in the family.

"I tell you what. I'll buy you a ticket home, pay for the test, and we can revisit once the baby is here and you know."

She sucks in a gasp. "You would miss the birth of your baby!"

"Not if it's not my baby."

She stands, planting her hands on my desk. "But it *is* your baby. You can have your DNA test to prove it, but you'll regret all your life missing his birth if he is yours."

My throat tightens, picturing a little boy running around Central Park, climbing the Alice in Wonderland statue, tossing a ball around. "It's a boy?"

"I think so. I did the string test."

What? "The string test?"

"Yes, you put a weight on a string and see if it goes back and forth or in circles."

Motherfucking unbelievable. "Did you even see a doctor?"

"Of course. There are programs for mothers. I applied for WIC."

"You qualified for WIC?"

"I live in a yurt and sell goat cheese. Yeah, I qualify."

Jesus. What have I gotten myself into?

"Do you even have enough money to get by?"

She hesitates. "I will. Eventually. When I can teach yoga again."

"What will you do with the baby during yoga?"

"He can come, too."

"And the goat?"

"She stays at the yurt. There's plenty to forage."

"You really live in one?"

She smooths her skirt. Damn, that's a big belly. "Most of the year. It gets too cold in the winter."

I ignore the fact that my dick seems to be interested in her roundness. Surely this is not a fetish I didn't know about. God help me. "Where do you go in winter?"

She seems uncertain, pressing the goat's head to her thigh. The hay is all gone. "I used to stay with April and Summer…" She trails off as if this is the first time she's realized she won't have a safe home for herself and the baby once the cold hits.

"Okay, okay. Let me think." I run my hand over my face. The only sure thing here is that I did indeed sleep with her eight months ago. "When are you due?"

"September 20. First babies can be late, though."

It's late August. We have less than a month to figure this out. "Where is your family? Your parents?"

She frowns. "My grandmother died when I was fourteen. My parents are not an option."

"What happened with them?"

She drops back into the chair. "They're part of what's wrong with society."

I feel another one of her rants coming on. They probably use pesticides. Or refuse to recycle. She's not going to like me any better. I like my steaks rare and my Ferrari full of gas. This is a hell of a mess.

But it's only a month. Uncle Sherman would kick my ass if he found out I booted a pregnant woman. My dad, too. And my mom would come in behind.

"I'll have Devin find a place for you. We'll get you an obstetrician here. When the baby's born, we'll do the test. Does that work?"

"What about Matilda?"

"Who's Matilda?"

"My goat."

Fuck. That'll be a tall order. "Let me get Devin in here."

She nods, then frowns at the floor by her feet. "Do you have a towel?"

Now I really do jump out of my chair. "Did your water break? Are you bleeding?"

She laughs. Actually laughs. Like any of this is funny. "No. Matilda is too full. I need to milk her. Do you have a bucket? Or a big jar?"

Jesus Christ. I've fucked up this time.

# 3

## LUCY

He's worse than I remember.

Court's big, fancy office has a private bathroom, so I lock myself inside it with Matilda. He's being condescending, and he and his assistant Devin are deciding my life for me, looking up Airbnbs and pet friendly hotels.

When they discussed the possibility of pretending Matilda is a dog on the reservations, I left them to come in here. Who do they think Matilda is, Scooby-Do? Are they going to dress her like a baby and stick her in a carriage?

That's not a bad idea, actually.

I'm glad to have a moment alone. It's been a long journey on the road, with heat and dirt and days and nights in trucks.

I'm grateful for every helpful person who got me to New York, but I'm so so tired. It's as though all my energy got used up, and now I'm sitting on a rug in a black-tiled bathroom with nothing left to run on.

There is much to do. I lift an empty soap dish by the faucet, inspect it for cleanliness, wash and dry it anyway, then fill it with feed for Matilda.

While she's busy with that, I remove the diaper, flush the contents, and swiftly wash it out with my goat milk soap. I clean up Matilda with it, rinse the cloth again, and hang it alongside the bamboo fleece diaper liner on a towel rack.

Everything in here is pristine. Before Matilda can do anything on the expensive-looking rug, I quickly pull out my spare diaper and liner and cover her again.

She's finished the feed. I don't dare let her drink from the toilet. I'm sure all manner of horrible chemicals are used to clean it.

I search under the sink and find the best thing, an industrial-sized bucket.

It's probably also been used with chemicals, so I set to scrubbing it with scalding water and my natural soap. My hands turn red, but I can't compromise with Matilda.

When it seems safe, I fill the bucket with fresh, cool water and let her drink as long as she wants. Then I wash it again and kneel next to her.

"Time to get that milk out of you, sweet girl."

She's filled to bursting, so once the smooth, creamy milk starts flowing, it's an easy job. She closes her eyes, no doubt relieved to be clean and fed and emptied.

At last, it's done.

The bucket is half full, but I don't know what to do with the milk. I set it on the counter by the sink.

I'm so tired. So tired. Matilda is, too. Goats don't

need as much sleep as humans, but it's been a long haul for both of us. She stays standing, which tells me she's nervous, even in our private space, but her eyes drift closed.

I sit cross-legged next to her. I should go out to the office again. See what they've figured out for me. I hate being at their mercy, but I'm at the end of my rope.

Court seems to think he'll be rid of me after the birth, but I know my history. He was one noteworthy night in a long, uneventful period of my life.

Matilda must decide that this place is okay, as she kneels to lie on the rug.

I rest my head on her fuzzy belly. She smells good, like natural soap and fresh milk.

I'll just take a minute to gather my thoughts…

*BAM BAM BAM.*

I startle awake at a pounding on the bathroom door.

"Lucy? LUCY? Are you okay?"

Court sounds worried. Or frustrated. Maybe mad. I don't know.

I sit up. I really was tired.

"Hold on," I say.

It feels way too hard to haul myself up, so I crawl to the door, unlatch it, and swing it open.

He bends down in front of me. "My God, did you fall? Are you injured?"

I push my sweaty hair out of my face. "No. I fell asleep."

Court glances around the bathroom. "Is that *milk* by my sink?"

Of course it is. Why must he keep pointing out the

obvious? "Would you like it? I have no way to store it currently." I feel more awake and grab the doorframe to heave myself up.

"Jesus Christ," Court says, reaching for my waist. "Let me help."

I'm glad he does, because the big movement of standing after sleeping causes the lightning cramps to flash through my midsection. I bend over, breathing through the pain.

"Is it time?" Court asks.

I hold up a finger. "No." I let out a long, slow breath. "It's the strain on the round ligaments around my belly. It's why I had to quit yoga. Why I came here."

He still has an arm around me, strong and tight. The fabric of his suit is soft and scented like clean linen. I feel protected for a moment. It's been a long time since I didn't have to stand solely on my own two feet.

Court and I didn't have much time together, but I remember it clearly. Impassioned. Furtive. Intense. I thought about it in the nights afterward, wondering if we should have stayed in touch.

But then I recalled his gruffness. The ease with which he took off from the room. There hadn't been any laughter or fun between us. Court was all business. Good business. He made sure all the deeds were checked off, like a task list. But it was still business.

When I found out I was pregnant, April took to her phone, searching up Court and the Pickle family and New York based on the scant details we had.

She determined he was a scoundrel based on the pictures of him with other women. And he never smiled.

"No good for our baby," she said then. "We don't need him." Summer agreed.

We had a plan. We would trade night shifts. Hand sew clothes. Make pottery and take walks in the woods. Homeschool, for sure. Teach the baby to garden and to love all living things.

But their lives moved on. I don't hear from them. I probably would. We've been friends since high school. But I don't have a phone or a computer or even an address.

My yurt is situated in the woods on the property of one of my yoga students, a middle-aged woman with a lot of land. I pay her in goat cheese. Sometimes I babysit her chickens. She lets me have eggs, too.

That feels far away in New York. Court's arm is gentle, possibly kinder than our first encounter. Surely there's more to him than what I saw then, or what we could glean online.

I realize I made a mistake thinking I should do this without him. The baby is his, too.

"Should I call an ambulance?" Devin asks. He's shorter and less built than Court, but he's smartly dressed in a shiny blue suit. His round glasses make him seem friendlier, but I'm not sure yet. He wants to lie about Matilda.

"I'm okay," I say. "It's a big baby in a small space."

Court leads me to a sofa. "Let's sit you down."

I do, but the softness of the cushion bends me too far, which sets off the cramps again. I gasp and clutch my belly.

"I'd feel better calling an ambulance," Devin says.

"Please don't," I get out. "I'll be okay if I can stretch out a moment."

Court lifts my feet onto the burgundy sofa. "Devin, adjust it near your end."

Devin stacks the soft pillows against the arm of the sofa.

My head sinks into them like a cloud.

"I'll be fine," I say. "I'm used to it. It's only a few weeks more." I can't stifle my yawn.

Something nudges my hand. It's Matilda. She presses her nose into my palm. "Shhh, my baby," I say.

She settles down on the floor beside the sofa.

"We should get her something to eat," Court says. "Go to that all-natural place on the corner."

"I'm vegetarian," I say.

"Right. Order a bunch of things. And get some bottles for that milk. I can store it in the fridge."

"No plastic," I say. "I'd rather pour it down the drain than put it in plastic."

Court frowns. "Glass bottles."

Devin nods. "Got it. Text me if you think of anything else." He takes off like the room is on fire.

My fingers trail along Matilda's back. "Precious girl. It was a long ride."

"I bet." Court looks down at us, hands shoved in his pockets. "Just sit tight. We'll figure things out. That's what I pay people to do."

I want to ask him if he has friends to talk to about this. It's going to be an adjustment. Maybe his brothers will be able to give him advice. I remember them being there that night, laughing and smacking his shoulder in encouragement when I approached.

That moment is crystallized in my memory. I wore a silvery dress, borrowed from Summer. Her shoes were a size too large, but I managed in them, crossing the strange little bar to say hello.

My first words to him had been, "What's a guy like you doing in a haunted bar like this?"

It's a lot, finding out that the night created a baby with a stranger. I've had time to come to terms with it. April, Summer, and I spent long hours discussing our future with the baby. It had been April who tied the string to a crystal and swung it over my belly.

They had been my friends. My future. I never expected to be doing this alone.

But I can't think about it any longer.

I'm simply.

Too.

Tired.

# 4

## COURT

She's out again.

I pace the room, eventually shucking my coat and tie. Is it warm in here? I turn down the air conditioning, then worry she'll be cold. I don't have a blanket.

But we have some downstairs. I pick up my office phone and scan the department list printed on the base. Merch is 4578.

I dial the number.

"Pickle merchandizing. This is Dawn."

"Dawn, we have blankets in the storeroom, right?"

"Oh! Mr. Armstrong. Yes, we do. Gosh. Did you want some?"

I backtrack. Slow down. Be polite.

"Yes. Thank you, Dawn. I appreciate you helping me out."

"Of course."

"Bring me two. Uh, please. And tell me about our drinkware. Do we have anything that isn't plastic?"

Her voice is bright. "Sure. We have aluminum and double-walled glass."

"Do the glass ones close?"

"Yes, they are twenty-ounce water vessels with a screw top."

"Great. Bring a whole case if you have them."

"To your office?"

"Where else?" Jesus.

Then I catch myself. Damn. The performance reviews loom in my vision. *Low work morale.*

I draw in a breath. "You are being very helpful, Dawn. If you could have someone bring up two blankets and what glass bottles you can spare, I would appreciate it."

"I'll do it myself."

"Thank you."

I drop the receiver onto the base with a sigh.

I never was grace under pressure. Not like Axel. Give him a challenge, and he'd rally everyone behind him, smiling the whole time. Nadia, too, our baby sister. They are both natural-born leaders, like Uncle Sherman.

Rhett and I fall on the sourpuss end of the scale. We don't like fuss or muss or pointless meetings or small talk. Rhett struggled too, down in Florida with the Dougherty division, but he seems to have pulled things out. He was more chipper when I saw them all on New Year's.

Then they deserted me when Lucy approached.

Lucy. Lucy what, I wonder. We're still on a first-name basis.

I swivel in my chair to look at her. She's softer in sleep, her hair a brown-gold cloud on the dark pillow. She has curled her hand protectively on her belly. The other dangles over the edge to rest on the head of the white goat.

She oozes maternal instinct.

Is she going to be the mother of my firstborn?

I text my fellow grump in the family.

*Me: You got a sec?*

*Rhett: Sure, bro. You at work?*

*Me: Yeah, but it's not a work thing.*

*Rhett: Lay it on me.*

*Me: Remember that woman I met at the Castle on New Year's?*

*Rhett: Silver dress? Country girl vibes?*

*Me: She hitchhiked from Colorado to New York to find me.*

*Rhett: What!*

*Me: With a goat.*

*Rhett: Holy shit. Why?*

*Me: She's eight months pregnant.*

*Rhett: Oh, damn.*

*Me: Exactly.*

*Rhett: You do a paternity test?*

*Me: She wants to wait until the baby is born.*

*Rhett: Are you having her stay with you?*

*Me: Not a chance. Devin's looking for a place.*

*Rhett: Damn.*

*Me: I feel blindsided.*

*Rhett: Where is she now?*

*Me: Sleeping in my office.*

*Rhett: She seem… okay? Not… you know.*

*Me: Off her rocker?*
*Rhett: I watched Baby Reindeer.*
*Me: No, not like that.*
*Rhett: What are you going to do?*

How to answer that? I was hoping he would have a suggestion.

There's a tap at my door.

*Me: Someone's here. Later.*

Rather than call out and wake Lucy, I hurry to the door and open it.

A young woman stands outside, two blankets stacked on a box.

My instinct is to grab them from her and walk away, but I force myself to smile. I speak in a low voice. "Thank you…" Shit. I already forgot her name.

"Dawn." She drops her voice too, looking around as if to figure out why.

Yeah, we don't need that. I open the door wider to take the box from her, but before I realize her intent, she enters the office and sets it on my desk.

When she turns around, her eyes get big. "Is that… a goat?"

And there it is. I can feel the annoyance rising. "Yes."

"And a pregnant woman?"

Anger rises. If she talks, I'll be the source of gossip. All courtesy goes out the window. My voice is a low growl. "You may leave. And use discretion like your job depends on it. Because it does."

Dawn sucks in a breath. "Okay… sir. I'll be quiet about it."

There's a gasp from the corner, then, "Court!"

I whip around to see Lucy struggling to sit up.

My voice is a boom. "Shouldn't you be resting?"

"Not while you're being mean to this poor woman!" She pushes on the side arm of the sofa to try to get upright.

Dawn lunges forward. "Let me help you. I remember those days. It's like being strapped to a bowling ball."

"This sofa eats you," Lucy says.

Dawn helps her sit up, "I hated soft cushions. You bend too far."

"Exactly! Can you help me stand?"

Dawn grasps Lucy's hands and braces herself to pull Lucy up.

"I like your goat," Dawn says.

"Her name is Matilda. I have fresh milk if you'd like some."

Dawn glances back at the box. "Is that why Mr. Armstrong wanted the glass-lined cups?"

They both seem to finally remember I'm also in the room.

"Yes," I say, stepping behind my desk.

"You got glass cups?" Lucy hurries for the box. "That would be perfect! I just need to wash them."

The women open the carton and pull out tall green cups with the words "Dill With It" screen-printed on the sides.

"These are hilarious," Lucy says. She turns to give Dawn a hug. "Thank you so much."

She seems perfectly recovered from whatever happened earlier.

Suspiciously recovered.

My eyes narrow. Am I being played here?

Lucy leans close to Dawn. "Does he always look like Grumpy Cat?"

Dawn bursts into giggles, but she straightens her expression quickly when she sees me glaring at her. "Mr. Armstrong takes Pickle Media very seriously."

"Did he threaten your job a minute ago?"

Dawn sobers instantly. It's about time she remembers who signs her checks. She hands Lucy the cups she's holding. "I have to go. Please, do come find me if you need anything else. I have a baby girl, six months old. I know exactly what you're going through."

The two women hug like they're old friends. It's been precisely four minutes since Dawn entered the room.

What is with this instant bonding?

Dawn releases Lucy and hustles out to the hall.

Lucy sets down one of the cups and inspects the other. "What did she ever do to you?"

I glower at her, but Lucy pays no attention. She lifts the blankets from my desk and turns to the sofa, then back to me. "Were these for me?"

"The air conditioning is strong."

"Huh." She sets them on a chair, instantly drawing the goat.

"She's going to eat that."

Lucy ignores me to pop the lid off the top of the cup and sniff inside. "Nice. No petroleum products. I can work with these." She fills her arms with a half-dozen of the cups. "Watch Matilda while I wash them."

It's not a question.

She disappears into the bathroom.

I stare at the goat, who has decided the blankets are not worth trying to eat. She looks at me, then in a wild, unexpected lunge, she jumps onto the desk.

I leap backward. What's happening here? "Lucy!"

She pops her head into the room. "Oh, goats like to find high spots. She's commanding the space."

Then she disappears again.

I snatch up my keyboard before it gets trampled.

The goat walks across the surface, slipping occasionally, leaving scratches on the wood and tearing loose papers. So much for my reports.

Then she stands stock still, like she's a statue guarding a town square.

She doesn't move.

I don't move.

I'm no longer sure whose office this is anymore.

## 5

## LUCY

That man is a real peach. And by peach, I mean the hard, sour ones that never ripen.

Grandma BeeBee compared people to produce all the time.

*Skinnier than a string bean.*

*Bitter as a winter lemon.*

*Hard-headed as a coconut.*

Do I really want to be saddled with that man for eighteen to life?

I need a friend or six. All I've got is an unborn child and Matilda. Neither one is a great conversationalist.

I'm thankful for something to do. After I fill the cups with milk and organize them in Court's mini fridge, I have no excuse to hide from him. I sit in one of the chairs since the sofa tries to eat me.

Court is super useless, constantly on his phone, scowling at whoever is talking to him, as if they can see his displeasure. Disdain. Dislike. That man is all *dis*.

He's moved to a round table in the far corner of his

office because Matilda has decided his desk is her domain. I think it's hysterical and haven't stepped in to move her from her perch.

As if I could. Once Matilda chooses a spot as hers, just let it go. Make a wrong move, and she'll *butt you with her head.*

Yeah, even girl goats get it on like that if you cross them.

If Court doesn't like it, he can bite me.

Actually, I might like him to bite me. I was hit with a wave of *jump-me-daddy* within minutes of walking into his office. I wanted to dig my fingers into that thick hair and straddle him on that big office chair—and oh, here I go again.

The need is as swift and hard as an ocean wave tossing me on my back.

Like I wish he would.

I've heard pregnant women get wild and woolly with the hormones, but I haven't felt it much until now.

And with all my chores done, the milk tucked away, Matilda clean and dry, all I have to do is sit in this chair with my feet propped up and watch him scowl.

It's kind of hot, if you're looking for a sulky bit of man-meat.

I might be.

Dang. I'm ramping myself up like I'm in heat.

And I've seen a lot of animals in heat.

Nobody acts right when they're on the prowl.

I close my eyes to get his flashing eyes and perfectly trimmed beard out of my vision. My belly rumbles so loud that Court stops talking.

"I have another engagement," he says abruptly and slams the office phone onto its base. He has no less than three of those phones in the same room. What a waste of resources.

"You didn't even say goodbye," I tell him, setting my feet on the ground.

He only grunts at that, rapidly typing on his phone. "It's been an hour since Devin left. The natural food store is only a block away."

"Maybe he ran for the hills. You're as bad as the goats in rutting season."

"I assume you're referring to reproductive copulation."

Did he really say that? Reproductive copulation?

I'm overcome with giggles. We already *did* that.

I can barely speak through my laughter. "I meant ramming each other with their heads."

He pierces me with a blue-eyed gaze. Will our son have blue eyes? Or my brown ones? Blue is recessive, but Grandma BeeBee had them.

Thinking of her calms me. I can picture her in the Colorado foothills, pulling roots for home remedies. She was the best member of my family.

Court's phone buzzes. "It seems he kept looking for glass bottles. I forgot to tell him I'd figured that out."

"I love that they're in 'Dill With It' cups. Appropriate."

He turns his cell over in his hands. "Are you suggesting that it applies to our situation?"

"I was thinking about Matilda stealing your desk. But, sure. Maybe it does."

He won't look me in the eye. And I get it. My appearance is life changing. He hasn't come to terms with it yet. And he won't for a while. I was in shock for a week.

But then Court surprises me by leaving the table and dropping into the chair next to mine.

Matilda stares down at us from her perch like a great goat goddess.

He tucks his cell phone in his shirt pocket. "Why didn't you let me know before you got this far along?"

*Now* he has questions. "Summer and April were going to raise him with me. We didn't need you."

He shifts in his chair, elbow propped on the leather arm, looking like the cover of a men's magazine. Well, other than the chewed-up bit of the cushion. Dang it, Matilda!

"So in that scenario where you raised the baby with your girlfriends, I never needed to know."

"Nope."

"And what about the child? Wouldn't there eventually be questions about a father?"

"Nah. Lots of kids have two moms. This one would have had three."

"Were you in a… relationship with these women?"

"I've known them since we were kids. We were best friends."

Or so I thought. I didn't expect the sudden abandonment. My throat feels thick. I hate crying, but I've been doing it constantly lately. The emotions go too deep, like stepping off your porch after a long, hard snow and sinking in straight to your armpits.

Court observes me sniveling and wiping my nose like a toddler who dropped her ice cream. "You never struck me as someone who cries a lot."

"You knew me for two hours, tops."

"Fair enough. You were just so fervent in your beliefs. You didn't leave any room for debate."

The hard chair is making my back ache. I shift sideways. "I don't allow for debate on my beliefs."

"And what are your beliefs?"

That's a question. "I don't know where to start."

He sits back, his hands steepled together. "Who influenced you?"

I get a sneaking suspicion he's preparing to pick me apart. If I talk about the environment, he'll talk about industry. If I talk about being vegetarian, he'll bring up all the ranchers.

I'm not interested in getting into a fight with him.

"Was it your parents?" He won't let it go.

I stall, making fairy braids in my hair, the kind that don't need bands at the bottom to stop them from unraveling.

He watches my fingers deftly work the strands. The unanswered question looms between us, growing like a balloon about to pop. He's good at silent pressure.

Thankfully, Devin returns with a load of brown paper bags. "I got four entrees, a sandwich, two salads, and two kinds of fresh-squeezed juice." He stops short when he spots Matilda on the desk. "What's happening?"

Court waves him to the corner. "Put it all on the table. I'm sure Lucy is starving."

I give him my most stern look. "That's it?"

They both turn to me. "You wanted more?" Court asks.

"No, no! I mean, that's all you have to say to Devin?" I turn to the man. "Court doesn't thank you for what you do?"

Devin shrugs and unpacks his purchases. "It's my job."

"But he can be courteous. It's literally his name. Court. Courtesy."

The two men exchange a glance.

This is ridiculous. I pop out of the chair, the smell of food drawing me to the table like a honeybee to a flower.

"I'm making a new rule," I say, picking up one of the juice cups and popping the lid. It must have been a proper store, because the containers are all recycled cardboard.

"Are you now?" Court asks. "Do enlighten us."

I take a sip and nearly swoon as unbridled sugar splashes into my empty belly. "Hold on a second."

I drink more, trying not to gulp, bordering on a brain freeze as the icy juice invigorates my bloodstream. This is heaven.

When I manage to force myself to stop, I set the half-empty cup on the table. "The new rule is that every time you forget to thank Devin for performing a task, he gets an hour off. I'll keep track."

I peer into a paper bag, not missing Devin's tight smile. He's trying not to cackle. I can tell.

"I won't agree to that," Court says.

"I think you will." I pull out a plump sandwich filled with hummus and greens and avocado on thickly sliced bread.

The men watch me as I unwrap the paper from a corner and take a big chomp. I can't stop the low moan that escapes as I eat it. It's so good. My belly quivers for a second. I'm so relieved to have it.

"And why do you think I'll do anything you say?" Court asks.

I swallow my bite, contemplating taking another before I answer. But I don't. I sit in a chair, spreading the waxy paper on the table to admire the sandwich.

When I turn to face the room, the men are watching, and so is Matilda, her nose in the air. She's clearly trying to decide between leaving her favorite spot and investigating my meal.

I pat my thigh, and she leaps down, startling Court into jumping out of his chair.

The papers under her hooves fly behind her, catching on the waves of air conditioning and fluttering through the room.

I pull out a big leaf of lettuce from the bread and hold it down to Matilda.

As the pages settle to the floor, I tell them, "Because somebody needs to work on this fixer-upper. Everyone will support me on this."

"What fixer-upper?" Court asks.

He genuinely doesn't get it.

So I tell him.

"You."

# 6

## COURT

If Lucy thinks she's converting me to her impractical, judgmental, all-granola, off-the-grid lifestyle, she can ride out of here on that pain-in-the-ass goat she arrived with.

Devin makes a strategic exit as I storm throughout the office, picking up the papers that wound up on the floor.

I can't make phone calls without her disapproving gaze. I can't hold meetings in here with her goat overlord.

And Devin leaves without any updates on the progress in finding a home for her.

I shove the mangled pages into my drawer and clear the desk for the inevitable return of the goat. Lucy has chomped into her sandwich with gusto and pays me no mind.

Time for a temporary exit. I step outside of that hellscape, carefully closing the door. Can't have the goat getting out.

Devin looks up from a spread of printouts.

"What's the progress in finding her a place to stay?" I ask.

"I had Angelique keep looking while I was gone." He neatly stacks the printouts with images of cabins and barns. "She brought me these in order of likelihood."

There are quite a few pages. That's promising. "Just choose one and make it happen."

"Are you okay with her being upstate?"

I hesitate. "What do you mean?"

"If we admit to having a goat, there's no place in Manhattan."

"How far?"

Devin shuffles through the papers. "Warwick. Patterson. Syracuse."

"Syracuse? That's hours away."

"You want her close?"

"Not necessarily." I gesture for him to keep talking.

"There are some goat farms with spaces you can rent. Some are B&Bs, others cabins." He glances up. "Warwick is the closest at an hour and a half. There's not a lot of options. Places are rare and often booked out."

"You think she'll go for that?" I ask.

"She loves her goat."

"Which one is that?"

"A dedicated goat farm. Halson Family Farm. It has tiny houses to rent. There's goat yoga. A whole barn and milking operation. Should be right up her alley."

"Print out some nice pictures of it. We'll convince her. Get her out of here."

Devin's face is pinched as he stacks the papers. "We'll have to find a doctor out there. What if she expects you to be involved?"

"She called me a damn fixer-upper. We're completely incompatible."

"But if she's having your baby."

"If it's mine, we'll work custody out with lawyers like any civilized set of parents with irreconcilable differences."

Devin's face is a mask of disapproval.

I sigh. "What?"

"You've been concerned about morale. Leadership. Company culture. She could help."

"How? By parading around barefoot with her goat?"

"I'm just saying, I think she could make you seem softer. More people oriented."

"No. Hell no. Send her to Warwick."

He stares down at the printouts. "Yes, sir."

God, I hate it when he reverts to formal talk, like I'm his military commander.

I turn around to return to my office, then decide, no, I don't want in there, either.

The conference room. I'll hole up in there with a phone and my laptop.

Except my laptop is in my office.

"Need something else?" Devin's voice is dark. He's annoyed with me. It's not unusual. Most people are.

"Would you please retrieve my laptop?"

"No."

I whirl around. "Why not?"

"I haven't completed your last task. I'm printing

pretty pictures to convince that perfectly nice woman to get out of your hair. And I don't like it. Plus, you owe me an hour off."

As if I'm following Lucy's cockamamie idea. "Never mind," I tell him.

I'll work from my phone. My files are all on a cloud drive.

I only take three steps when a heavy thud rattles my office door.

What now?

Devin and I look at each other.

Then there's another one.

Is it Lucy? Is she having pains again and can't open the door?

I yank on the handle and throw the door wide.

A white fuzzy head rams my knees, knocking me backwards. I fall on my ass, my head barely missing Devin's desk.

The goat takes off down the hall.

I scramble to my feet to follow it, then a wild flash of color crashes into me.

Good God. It's Lucy, and I've tripped her. I cradle her to stop her fall.

We make a slow-motion descent to the shiny floor. I carefully hold her up so that my shoulder takes the brunt of the landing.

"Are you okay?" I ask.

"Yeah. Are you?" Her eyes are wild.

"The goat is gone," Devin says.

Both Lucy and I look up from our position on the floor. We can hear the surprised cries down the hall.

"Matilda!" Lucy fights to disentangle herself from me and push to standing. But she no more gets to her knees when she grabs her belly. "Oh, these stupid pains!"

"Whoa, whoa." I scramble upright and lift her to her feet. "Take it easy."

"I'm a very self-sufficient woman!" Her face is red as she pokes my shirt. "Now let me go get my baby!"

She tries to take off, but I hold her shoulders. "You need to think about *our* baby."

"Oh, *now* it's yours." She shakes herself loose from me. "Let go!"

I release her, and she takes off in a run-walk, both hands holding her belly like it's about to bounce off her body.

Staff members have come to their doors to watch the commotion.

"We're all right," I say. "Just a situation with a goat."

I catch the murmurs as I follow her.

"Is she pregnant?"

"Does she not have any shoes?"

"What does he mean, a goat?"

I hate this. Fucking hate it. I take off in a sprint, quickly overtaking Lucy.

"Get my goat!" she calls after me.

Oh, yes, I'm definitely going to get her goat.

We arrive at the elevator bank. Several shocked and laughing people stand there, peering down the hall. One of them is my VP of advertising, Brent.

"You looking for a goat? Yay high?" He holds out his arm.

The woman behind him points across the elevators to the other hall. "It ran past us."

The building is a letter "H" of hallways, with the elevator bank as the bridge between them.

I rush beyond the onlookers, but on the other side, I'm not sure which way it went. I pause, my dress shoes squeaking on the glossy floor.

Then I hear a roar of voices to my right.

That way.

I take off again. The individual offices in this hall are all closed up, but the corridor ends in an open section of cubicles.

When I get to the large room, a dozen employees have circled up by the back wall.

Hopefully, they've cornered it.

I slow down, straightening my jacket and checking my hair. I don't like to appear disheveled or flustered.

Among the tech support crew, I recognize Ian, the supervisor.

"Everything all right?" I ask as if I haven't been chasing livestock through Pickle Media.

He looks up. "You know anything about this?"

"About what?" I attempt to nonchalantly rest my elbow on a nearby shelf, but it's less sturdy than I expect, and it tilts, sending a cascade of white binders crashing to the floor.

The noise draws everyone's attention, and I see a flash of white.

She *was* in there, and now, they've let loose of her again.

The pain in the ass interloper thinks she'll duck by

46

me again, but as she navigates the narrow lanes between cubes, I throw myself in her way.

"I wouldn't do that!" someone says right as her hind legs kick out, nailing me in the balls.

I can't stop my long, rather impressively loud, "Fuu-uuuck" from drawing everyone's attention a second time. I drop to my knees.

"She doesn't have a leash or anything," Ian says, run-skipping around my body to go after her.

Several others follow him. I can't move yet, the fire in my groin showing no signs of ebbing.

A woman approaches. "Are you okay, Mr. Armstrong?"

I nod. "Go find the goat."

"Who does she belong to?" she asks.

I don't even know how to explain that. I wave her on. "Just go."

Only when the cubes have cleared out, the entire tech department disappearing down the hall, do I let out another squeal of pain.

That damn goat.

This damn day.

It's never going to end.

## 7

## LUCY

The pain darting around my oversized belly gets more manageable as I pass the elevators and turn toward the noise that I'm pretty sure means Matilda has gone that way.

When I turn into a new hallway, I spot her! She races toward me like hell is on her heels.

I kneel and scoop her into my embrace. She trembles like a newborn.

"Poor baby girl. Are you okay?" I stroke her head.

She startles as the thunderous pound of feet approach in the hall. There must be a dozen people in khakis barreling toward us.

Matilda tenses like she might take off again, but I hold her firmly.

"Everyone stop!" I call out. "Think of this sweet girl!"

And they do, bunching up together several yards away like a human accordion.

When the hall has quieted, I turn Matilda to face them. "Matilda, these are the wonderful workers of Court's company. I'm sure we'll get to know them all."

I look up at them. "You can introduce yourselves one at a time. That's all she can handle."

They look at each other as if unsure of what to do.

"Come on now. Matilda never forgets a smell. If she likes you, she'll put her head down. If she's glaring at you, watch out, because she might butt you with her head."

This sends a ripple of laughter through the hall.

A young woman in a gray skirt approaches first. Her chin-length hair slides forward as she bends down to extend a hand to Matilda. "Hello, Matilda, I'm Penny."

Matilda lowers her head and allows Penny to scratch between her ears.

"Lovely. Matilda likes you."

"She's adorable."

"Thank you."

A young man is next, all khakis and smiles. "Matilda! How's it hanging?" He extends a fist for her to sniff like she's a dog.

Matilda looks at him for a minute, then lowers her head. He pats her between the ears.

Then Court reappears.

Matilda rears back on her hind legs.

"Whoa!" everyone cries, and their sudden burst of noise startles her even more.

I sigh, wishing I had the lead with its neck loop with me. I wrap my arms around her, but the effort gets me a new round of darting pains. They won't kill me or send me into labor. I know that. But it's not fun to deal with.

Penny rushes forward to help. "You're turning white," she says. "Let me hold her."

Matilda allows it.

One of the young men says, "I have a dog leash in my cube. Will that help?"

"Yes," I tell him. I sit against the wall, holding my belly. This is the worst. I've always been so strong, but since the third trimester began, I've been as fragile as a tomato plant.

Court steps back into the crowd. Without him visible, Matilda settles down.

The man returns with a blue leash. "It's an extra I bought and never took home," he says. "You can keep it."

"Thank you," I tell him.

Penny releases Matilda once it's fastened.

She darts forward as if to figure out if Court is back there.

Penny's gaze meets mine. "She really doesn't like Mr. Armstrong, does she?"

"They didn't have a good introduction," I say. "She'll get used to him."

The man reels Matilda back to us, and Penny kneels down to hold her.

"I think I forgot to say my name earlier. I'm Joe." He extends a hand.

I reach forward to shake it, suppressing the grimace as another darting pain zigzags over my middle. "Nice to meet you, Joe. And Penny."

"Are you new here?" Penny asks.

"Oh, no. I just know Court."

Joe and Penny exchange a glance.

I've said the wrong thing. "I mean, Mr. Armstrong."

"We know who you meant." Joe glances back at the dispersing crowd. "You're not the sort of person we would expect Mr. Armstrong to know."

Matilda climbs onto my lap, what little there is, and rests her head on my thigh. I stroke her ears. "What sort of people does he know?"

Joe and Penny exchange another glance. "We're not sure. Nobody knows him very well."

"We should fix that." The adrenaline starts to wane, and exhaustion threatens to take over. "I should get back to his office. I didn't finish my lunch."

"You were eating lunch in Mr. Armstrong's office?" Penny asks.

"Of course. Is that weird?" I carefully shift Matilda off my legs so I can try to stand. It won't be easy from the floor, not with this belly.

"No, no, of course not." Joe extends a hand, and I gratefully accept it.

A deep rumble of a voice comes from behind. "I've got it."

It's Court, and he doesn't look pleased. Matilda goes rigid, so I wrap my arms around her. "Now, now, girl. That's enough."

"I'll take her." Penny grasps the leash close to the collar and gently tugs Matilda away.

Joe releases my hand as Court bends down to put an arm around my shoulders. This is way more familiar than what Joe was attempting, and I can feel them looking at us as Court hauls me to my feet.

"I'm having his baby," I tell them. "But we're not a couple."

I feel rather than hear the growl in Court's throat. Oh, I shouldn't have said that.

When I'm upright, I shake Court off. "I'll take Matilda from here."

"You sure?" he asks.

"Absolutely." Normally, Matilda would walk easily by my side, but she has an issue with Court for some reason. So I leave her on the leash.

"Thank you both! I'm sure I'll see you again!" I wave behind me as I move down the hall, not waiting on Court. If I can keep Matilda from looking at him, she'll be easier to manage.

"Stop by I.T. anytime!" Penny calls.

I can feel Court's rage like a wall of heat pushing me forward. He's really mad. I walk more quickly as we pass the elevators.

It's quiet now, and only Devin waits in the hall outside Court's office. He moves from behind his desk without a word, opening the door.

"Please come with us," I whisper as I pass. I don't want to face the angry beast alone.

He waits for Court to enter, then follows us in and closes the door.

I tug Matilda to walk alongside me to the round table and bribe her to stay with another piece of lettuce.

We make it fewer than five seconds before Court roars, "Why did you say that?"

If this had been a cartoon, my hair would have blown back and all the food on the table would have fallen over.

But this is real life, and he's possibly justifiably mad that I spilled his business in front of Penny and Joe, who are probably telling everyone that the barefoot woman with a goat is pregnant with his illegitimate not-love child.

"I'm sorry," I say. "I shouldn't have brought up our relationship."

"You think?" Court paces the room, his hands clasped on his head.

"It was bound to get out anyway," Devin says.

"Like my goat?" I can't stop my giggle.

Devin quirks a smile but quickly straightens his expression when Court turns around.

"We haven't established that this is my child. Until it is legally handled, I would appreciate you keeping the alleged paternity to yourself."

"But *I* know," I insist. "You can require a piece of paper, and I get that, but I know. For a fact. Without a doubt."

He stomps around the desk and drops into his chair, angrily shaking his computer mouse to wake up the screen.

I glance at Devin, who shrugs. He sits near me, spreading out a sheaf of printouts. "I have some options for where you can stay while we wait on *Court's baby* to be born."

I beam at him. "Perfect. Let's take a look. And how many hours off does he owe you so far?"

"Three."

We both ignore the feral growl that comes from the other side of the room.

I have an ally.

Plus, two in I.T.

Lucy 3, Court 0.

## 8

## COURT

Despite quite a number of threats, Devin insists
that he has an unmovable appointment after
work. I'll need to be the one to take Lucy out to the goat
farm he booked.

I don't believe him for a minute, but my tyranny
over him only legally extends to his work hours.

He's already gone above and beyond today, even if
he appears to have sided with Lucy and the goat.

I don't drive my Ferrari to the office, and I don't
want that damn goat in it, anyway. So I call an Uber to
take us out. I completely forget to mention the goat, so
as I lead a barefoot Lucy and her livestock out to the
silver Altima who took the ride, the driver honks at me.

He rolls down the passenger seat window, and in a
heavy Brooklyn accent, says, "You think I'm letting that
goat in my car?"

I bend down. "Yes."

"Hell, no. I'm not having that creature make a mess
in here."

Lucy leans in. "Matilda is lovely. And she wears a diaper. There's no risk."

But the man takes off in a squeal of tires.

We jump back on the curb, Lucy pulling the goat close to her. "What a horrible man!" she cries.

I pull up the app and give him a one-star before canceling the ride. He could have said no without nearly running us over. "I'll try again."

She peers over my phone. "You probably want to use Uber Pet to get someone animal friendly."

I look up at her. "How do you know that?"

"I've used Uber."

"From your yurt with no cell phone?"

"No, when I went out drinking with friends. You're making assumptions about me."

"You showed up with a bag of hay and a goat."

"That doesn't mean I'm ignorant." She lifts her chin in defiance, and for one strange flash of a second, I think about kissing her.

Hell no to that. That's what got me into this mess.

I find the Uber Pet options. These have to be reserved in advance. I find one for an hour from now.

"We'll have to wait," I tell her, glancing down at her feet. "Why don't we get you some shoes?"

She shrugs. "I just need to fix mine. I haven't had a chance."

"Maybe you should have more than one pair."

She looks around at the buildings. "I have a feeling there isn't a pair of shoes anywhere near here that I could afford. I got these from a Buy Nothing group."

"What is that?"

"A neighborhood group where they trade items they no longer need instead of selling them."

"I'm buying you shoes."

She shrugs, and we take off down the street. We're an odd-looking bunch. Lucy with no shoes, a goat, and a leather knapsack with hay sticking out. Me, with no less than four green "Dill with it" soft-sided lunch coolers slung over my shoulder like I'm hawking stadium souvenirs at a game.

"You're sure the place doesn't have leather sofas?" Lucy asks as we pass store windows. "I couldn't sleep knowing there were skinned cows that close."

"No leather," I say, although I don't really know. It seems unlikely. I'll hedge my bets.

She unfolds the printout Devin gave her. "You're right. The pictures look like fabric. I don't know why I'm so worried. Ouch!" She pauses to pick up a metal pop-top lid to a can. "I'm lucky this didn't cut me."

Visions of tetanus shots dance in my head. "You're not hurt?"

She lifts her dirty, blackened foot. "Nope."

"It's not safe for you to walk around. Come over here."

She holds the lid in her hand as we move close to the wall. There aren't any trash bins on this block.

We're stuck. No shop in this area will let her try on shoes like this. I can't let her walk any farther. What a mess.

I lean my head against the wall, trying to think.

"Can't we take the subway out to the goat farm?" Lucy asks. "I was able to ride it fine."

"You got lucky." I check my watch. "Besides, it's rush hour, and it's more likely someone will take issue with your goat."

"Her name's Matilda."

I pull up a map app to see what's nearby. There has to be something we can do to pass the time, even with the goat. An outdoor cafe, maybe.

But I spot something a hundred times better. It's a wellness spa, offering holistic healing, meditation yoga, and earth friendly manicures and pedicures. It's only two blocks away.

Now we're getting somewhere. I punch the link to call them. I don't wait for a hello. "Can you do a pedicure right now? I'll triple the fee."

There's a breathy laugh on the line. "Welcome to Wenova's Wellness. I'm Kaliyah. Let me see if we can work you in."

Lucy feeds Matilda a handful of grain while I wait. Passersby in New York walk past us briskly, only a few glancing our way. This aspect of the city is coming in very handy at the moment. I can't stand being the subject of curiosity.

"All right, sir. Yes, we can see you. Are you nearby?"

"Two blocks. We'll head that way."

"Can I get a name?"

"Sure. Lucy. Lucy…" I realize I don't know Lucy's last name. She's kneeling in front of her goat, not paying me any mind. "Lucy Armstrong."

She hears that, though, and glances up, eyebrows raised.

"Is the number you called on a good one?" Kaliyah asks.

"Yes."

"We'll see you in a few minutes, then."

I pocket my phone. I'll send Lucy into the spa, get her cleaned up, find a shoe store. Then we'll get on the Uber Pet ride and… oh, damn.

The goat. What will I do with the goat?

"What was that all about?" Lucy asks.

"I got you an appointment at a spa while we wait."

"A spa? Like for facials?"

Now that's a word. If we'd done *that* instead of a condom, we wouldn't be here.

"A pedicure."

"But if they use chemicals…"

"No, it's all earth friendly. Right up your alley. We can pass time while we wait for the ride." I steer her back onto the sidewalk. "Are your feet feeling okay?"

"Yeah, sure. I walk barefoot in the woods all the time. I've built up good callouses."

This isn't a picture I want in my head.

We pass by a trash can, but Lucy hesitates to relinquish the tin lid. "It should be recycled."

"Just apologize to Mother Earth and move on."

Lucy frowns. "That's not how it works."

I snatch the tin lid from her and toss it.

Her frown deepens, and for a second, I think she might dig it out. She better not, because I can see at least three aluminum cans as well.

"That *is* how it works in New York. There are people

who make money by collecting the metals in the trash cans and turning it in."

"Really?"

"Absolutely. It'll be handled and help someone, too."

"Oh." She presses a hand to her cheek, her eyes misting. Seriously, more waterworks? "I like that."

"It's your good deed for the day." I take her arm and steer her toward the spa.

The moment we enter Wenova's Wellness, I know we're going to be fine. There are three cats, two dogs, and incredibly, a *goat* in the expansive front room, sitting in the window for passersby to admire.

The woman behind the desk stands. "Look at your Nigerian Dwarf!"

I recognize the voice from the phone. Kaliyah comes around to greet our goat. She's tall and picturesque with glowing black skin against a shiny gold dress and jewelry. "What's her name?"

Lucy beams. "Matilda. She's two years old."

"Has she been pregnant? Does she produce?" Kaliyah kneels to pet the goat's head.

"She does! I have several quarts bottled in those bags. I make cheese and soap."

"Oh, you'll have to give us your card. We're always looking for local goat milk providers. Are you Lucy?"

"I am."

Kaliyah returns to the counter. "Put your baby next to Simone. If they get along, it'll do Matilda good to have goat company while you get your pedicure."

I can't even keep up with this conversation. Goat

company? And did Lucy find herself a buyer for her products?

"Oh… I don't know." But even as Lucy says it, Matilda spots the other goat and trots over. Lucy drops the leash. The two goats size each other up, then butt heads good naturedly.

"Oh, look at them," Kaliyah says. "Simone is going to have such a wonderful time with her."

A diminutive woman in a blue smock arrives through a beaded curtain. "Lucy? You ready?"

She turns to me. "I guess I'll see you in a little while?"

I realize I'll be free of the goat. "Hey, what's your shoe size?"

"Seven, why?"

"Since there is goat bonding happening, I can run out and buy shoes."

Lucy frowns. "That's not necessary."

"It is. Now go get your pampering."

She hesitates but seems to realize she's holding up the woman waiting for her. "Be good, Matilda," she says and disappears through the curtain.

"You can leave the bags here if you like," Kaliyah says. "Would you like me to store them in a refrigerator?"

"Sure," I say, then inexplicably add, "She milked the goat a few hours ago. I've kept them in my office fridge."

"Oooh, nice and fresh. Simone doesn't produce anymore. They dry up if they go too long between pregnancies."

"I didn't know that."

She takes the bags from me. "You can wait on the sofa with the animals, if you like."

"No, no. I'm going to look for Lucy some new shoes. Do you have a recommendation? No leather. Natural stuff."

She smiles. "Of course. There's a Naturalist Outfitter three blocks down and around the corner to the right. You might want to hurry, though. They close at six."

"Got it. Should I settle this out? I was serious about paying triple."

She waves me off. "We can discuss it when she's done."

I head for the door, sidestepping the curious menagerie. I had no idea businesses like this existed.

Naturalist Outfitters is a small, bright store nestled between a deli and a pizzeria. I'm relieved to see an entire table of Birkenstocks.

"Can I help you?" A tall, ladle-thin man approaches in cargo shorts and a pale-yellow top with mesh sides.

"Those look like leather," I say, pointing to the table of shoes.

"They are. Birkenstocks are made of thick, all-natural leather."

"Are all Birkenstocks leather? My friend is opposed to animal textiles."

"They have vegan microfiber versions as well." He lifts a gray pair.

"I need that kind."

"We have the traditional style with the double strap,

a thong, as well as a crisscross design." He holds out each one.

The crisscross one is the most appealing, but probably Lucy is more practical.

Although she did say she went out drinking with friends.

"Do you have the crisscross ones in size seven?"

"Let me go look." He takes off for the back of the store.

I walk around. The store is highly eclectic, selling everything from clothes to jewelry to hammocks.

Lucy only has one knapsack with her. Given how much feed is in it, she may not have even packed any other clothes.

There's a yellow dress that I think would appeal to her. It's a tank style and is flowing and loose. It should accommodate her belly. I pull one off the rack and check the fabric tag. Cotton. That will work.

Then there's a T-shirt that reads, "My other dog is a goat," and I can't pass that up. I get a large one. Maybe she can wear it to sleep in. Then pink fuzzy socks with goats on them.

"We have them in both black and brown," the man says, setting two boxes on the counter.

"Which do you think goes better with this dress?" I ask, holding it up.

"Brown, I'd say."

I'd buy both colors, but I get the sense that Lucy has a limit to what she'll accept. "Let's go with brown, then. And these." I set my pile by the register.

"I'll ring them up." He opens a sturdy paper bag

and tucks the shoebox inside, then folds up the dress and shirt and socks to set inside.

"Did you see this?" He turns to the glass counter next to the register and opens the back. He pulls out a necklace that holds a locket shaped like a heart. A goat is etched into the front.

"I'll take it, too," I say, then wonder if I should have. It's jewelry.

But I pay for all of it and head out.

As I walk back to the spa with my bag, I realize that everything I know about Lucy is in this bag. She's pregnant. She likes goats. She's all natural and vegetarian. Her shoe size is seven.

The necklace box sits on top. It suddenly seems too personal. Not cute and funny, but the wrong message. Like I'm reaching out to her.

And I'm not.

I remove the box from the bag and tuck it in my suit pocket.

The last thing I need is for that woman to think we're anything but potential co-parents.

There were never two people more different than us.

# 9

## LUCY

T his is heaven.

The last time I got a pedicure, I was a teenager living at home with my parents.

Mom took me to a nail salon, aiming for mother-daughter bonding. It was tickly and a little embarrassing, my pants rolled up, my ugly feet exposed.

I've learned to love my pudgy, short toes and wide instep. My feet are good to me, taking me where I need to go. I've even traversed one of the biggest cities in the world, my tough, calloused soles never giving me any trouble.

Janet, the manicurist, consulted with me about how much of my well-toughened hide to remove. Apparently, they have booties full of treatment that will peel off layers of skin.

I said, "None."

And she'd understood, growing up on a farm herself, the value of tough feet.

But I got a good sudsy soak, warm paraffin treatment, and pretty pink polish. When she sits back, I lift my legs to admire them. My skin glows, and my nails sparkle. "I love it!" I tell her.

Kaliyah from the front desk comes in to check on us. "You're all done!" she says. "Simone and Matilda have settled in for a nap. You might have to wake them."

"Poor dears," I say. "Matilda didn't like the subway at all."

"The subway!" Kaliyah shakes her head, sending her dangly earrings to swinging. "We have to fetch our truck to move Simone around."

"Nobody bothered us, not really. But Court requested an Uber Pet for tonight. Do you think they'll take Matilda? The first driver took off."

"It's risky. We'll cross our fingers for you." She helps Janet put away her supplies. "I talked to our owner, Monique, about Matilda."

"What about her?" I set my feet on the floor, and the smooth coolness of the tiles feels like a brand-new connection with the earth.

"Since Simone isn't producing, Monique was wondering if you were selling milk, or maybe your soap. She'd like to talk about your ingredients."

"I'd be happy to."

"Here's her card. She did say she'd like to make an offer on the milk you have on you, if you have some to spare. She loves making cheese, and store supplies are always a few days old or more."

"I'd be happy to sell it to her. Did she have a price?"

"I'm authorized to negotiate that with you."

Kaliyah leads me down a hall to a breakroom.

"Court gave them to me to put in the fridge. I unpacked seven bottles. That's probably close to a hundred ounces."

"Yes, she produced quite a lot today since she was delayed."

Kaliyah opens the fridge to reveal the bottles. "Those are glass lined?"

"They are. I washed them with goat soap."

She reaches in and pulls one out, unscrewing the top. "May I take a sniff?"

"Absolutely."

Her eyes close dreamily as she takes it in. "This is perfect."

Janet leans in the door. "Her friend is back."

I reach out to Kaliyah. "It would mean a lot to me if I could pay for the pedicure with the milk and not have Court cover it. Is there a way we can barter? I can bring more milk if I need to cover the rest."

She nods. "How about we exchange it for the pedicure, including a cash tip for Janet? And you'll talk to Monique about providing more and negotiate a going rate? Maybe weekly?"

"Yes!" I'm giddy that I've already found a way to make a little money here. I know Court is covering my room at the goat farm, but this way, I can pay for Matilda's feed and food for myself. Maybe I can grow a few things on the farm or work on it and keep some vegetables.

"Perfect." Kaliyah opens a cabinet and pulls out a pair of glass pitchers with lids. "Let's empty your cups."

We quickly transfer the milk to pitchers and rinse out Court's bottles.

Kaliyah repacks them into the coolers, other than the one filled with my leftover food. "This is a great way to transport them."

It is. I'll have to ask Court if it's okay to keep these.

"Thank you so much." I impulsively give Kaliyah a hug, taking in the rich coconut and sage scent of her.

"I'll see you again when we get more milk."

"Yes!"

We head back to the waiting room. Court sits on a chair, a bag tucked between his knees. He stands and pulls out his wallet.

The sudden movement startles the goats, which sets the dogs to barking. The cats scurry out of the room, which causes Matilda to rear back.

She spots Court and runs toward him, head down. Simone is apparently on her side, because she's close behind.

"Matilda!" I call, but I'm too late. She rams Court's knees, knocking him back into the chair. Then Simone gives a second shot.

"Ladies!" Kaliyah calls. "Calm yourselves."

The two of us pull the goats away from Court, whose glare is murderous.

"I'm so sorry," Kaliyah says. "These two had their minds made up."

"I'm getting used to it." Court brushes goat hair off his knees. He opens his wallet.

Kaliyah raises her palms. "Lucy and I worked out a deal for her goat's milk. Her services are all covered."

"Oh. But I offered triple."

She sits at her desk. "We're all good here. Feel free to wait for your ride. We're open another hour."

"Thank you." I sit next to Court with the coolers in my lap. "I sold all the milk."

"That's great." He pushes the paper bag toward me with his shiny shoe, eyes on the goats. They're standing stock-still, staring at him. "I bought a few things you might need."

We trade bags, and I lift the fuzzy socks out of his. "How adorable. Kaliyah, look!"

"I love them," she says, her smiling eyes moving from the socks to Court.

"And the shirt!" I lift it and hold it over my chest. "My other dog is a goat!"

Then there's a pretty yellow dress. "Court! You shouldn't have!"

"Ladies need to be spoiled," Kaliyah says.

Oh, she has no idea what Court is really like. I can tell by her pleased expression that she thinks we're a happy couple, even if my goat hates him.

At the bottom is a shoebox. I'm hoping he didn't get the leather Birkenstocks. I worried about this as I got my pedicure, convincing myself it would be okay. I would thank the cow for her sacrifice and wear them, anyway.

But he's gotten the microfiber ones, in a style I haven't seen before. "They're so cute!" I slide my toe through the loop. "I can go dancing in these!"

I stand to show them off, tilting my feet and posing.

Matilda breaks her stare to turn to me.

"Look, Matilda!"

Matilda sniffs at my toes with their smell of products and new shoes.

I want to give Court a happy hug, but he's busily staring at his phone.

"Court?"

He looks up.

"Would it be okay if I hung onto the coolers and bottles for a while? They'll be great for transporting the milk until I can get a better solution."

"Sure. It's just merch."

"Okay."

He's already on his phone again.

"And, Court?"

He looks up.

"Thank you for the gifts and the shoes. They're the nicest things I've had in a while."

He grunts.

We're back to that. It's fine.

His phone buzzes. He frowns. "The ride's here. We'll see how it goes."

"Good luck," Kaliyah says. "If you need to wait on another one, or make other arrangements, feel free to return."

"You've been so lovely," I tell her.

I shoulder my knapsack but let Court take the shopping bag and coolers. When Matilda's leash is securely in my hand, we head for the door.

This ride is a minivan.

Court leads me to the back door. "Just jump in and say nothing, like it's perfectly normal to have a goat."

I nod.

He slides the panel. "Hello," he says to the driver, a heavyset man poking at the phone mounted to his dash.

"You Court?"

"I am."

I duck down behind Court to climb in. There are three rows, and the second-row seat is folded down, so I move to the very back and tug Matilda in behind me.

If she doesn't make any sounds, he might not notice she's a goat.

"Long ride," Court says. He returns the lowered seat to its place and sits in the middle row to block the driver's view of the back of the van.

The man looks up. "It'll take over an hour to get there."

"I'll be riding back to the city," Court says.

"Looks like my evening is set, then." He seems pleased.

Court closes the door, and I quietly feed Matilda bits of grain as we pull into traffic. If she stays quiet, we'll make it.

We're only a few minutes into the ride when I feel terribly sleepy.

It's been a long day since I got on the subway in Queens.

Matilda licks my hand until she's sure she's gotten every grain.

Then I rest one hand on my belly and the other on Matilda. I have leftovers to eat tomorrow. A goat farm to live on. A way to make a little money.

All is well in my world.

And I can't stay awake a minute more…

## 10

**COURT**

Pregnant women sure sleep a lot.

I glance back at Lucy as we enter the Lincoln Tunnel.

She's resting on her goat, which looks up at me with half-lidded eyes. They're both relaxed.

I let out a long breath. Things are finally going the right direction.

This is the first time I've been able to pause and think about this situation I've been thrust into.

Due to thrusting into her.

A baby?

With this woman?

My father, who delivered a threat-laden speech to me in high school about girls, protection, and always doing the right thing, will kick my ass.

Except I did use protection. And wasn't I doing the right thing?

As we get farther from the island, I begin to wonder.

Lucy is absolutely convinced the baby is mine. She's

announced it to everyone, which is a different, separate problem.

I still don't know her last name.

Devin should have put it on the rental when they got together to fill out the form. I flick my phone awake and find the email he forwarded from the farm.

Lucy Brown.

I google her to see what comes up, not sure what I'll find.

There's a Facebook profile, which surprises me since she seems to hate technology. I click on it.

She kept it up while in college, which is another unexpected detail. Based on what I've seen of her so far, shoeless, traveling with a goat, I wouldn't have expected her to manage coursework, computers, and being surrounded by people so unlike her.

But she graduated from the University of Boulder in —I read it three times to be sure.

*Finance?*

That would require software, spreadsheets, data.

So this all-natural lifestyle, the yurt, the yoga is all new.

Okay, not totally. There are check-ins at a yoga studio from way back. I scroll through what personal posts are public. They stop abruptly five years ago, right around when she would have graduated. She seems to be twenty-seven.

She had a boyfriend named Steve back then, one she never changed her relationship status with before abandoning the platform.

There are pictures of them, heads together, hiking outside of Denver. I recognize the trail.

A heaviness settles in my belly. What the hell is that? Jealousy of some five-year-old relationship that must have ended? Wishing he'd hung on to her, and I wouldn't be here?

I don't know.

The driver turns back to me for the first time since we got in. "We're about ten minutes out." He sniffs. "Smelly dog?"

Anything I say might be incriminating, so I just grunt.

I should wake Lucy before we get there. I reach over the seat to touch her knee.

She startles awake, looking disoriented. Only meeting the gaze of her goat settles her. "Are we there?"

"Almost." I realize once we separate, I have no way to contact her. That won't work. I make a quick decision. "Tomorrow, I'll have a cell phone delivered to you so you can search for an obstetrician that suits you. I'll have Uber installed with an account attached so that you can attend appointments."

"That sounds expensive."

"I'll cover the rides. And the doctor. Forward me the information once you determine who it is, and I'll arrange payment."

She stares out the window as she nods. "Will you come to any of the appointments?"

"That seems rather intrusive."

"They do sonograms. You can see the baby."

"You can forward those to me. Do you have an email address?"

She sighs. "Somewhere. I'll track it down. Or make a new one."

"My contact information will be in the phone." I consider asking her about the finance degree but don't want to admit to online stalking.

We're quiet as we travel down a small two-lane highway lined with trees. Sometimes I forget how close we are to expansive places when I'm deep in the city.

"It looks nice out here," Lucy says, "Lots of open space."

The driver slows as we approach a sign that says, "Goat Yoga at Halson Family Farm!"

Lucy touches the glass as if it's a fond memory. "Maybe I can do a few stretches with them. If I'm not teaching, I can do only the moves that don't strain my belly."

"Is that allowed?"

She shrugs. "I mean, getting around at all is already causing a lot of discomfort."

"You shouldn't be on bed rest?"

"There's no threat to the baby. Just pain for me. Pregnant joints get loose, and tendons can be overtaxed. Probably it's hereditary."

"Did it happen to your mom?"

"I have no idea." She keeps her gaze on the window as we turn through an open gate onto a long, winding road.

"Do your parents know about the baby?"

"No."

"Do you plan on telling them?"

"Maybe."

"What would change your mind?"

Her chin wobbles. Is she going to cry again?

"I'll have to be at my last resort."

"I thought that was me."

She turns her attention to the goat, stroking the fuzzy white head. I'm beginning to see that it serves as a support animal. "If you throw me out, I'll be forced to go to them."

"I wouldn't—" I cut myself off. The baby might not be mine. What will I do then? Pay for her to return to Colorado, I guess. Or her parents. Or maybe send her to whoever the real father might be.

"Oh, look!" She leans toward the door. "The goats!"

I bend down to peer outside. "Those are bigger than yours."

"They're Nubians! You can tell by their long, floppy ears."

I see that. "Are they friendly?"

"Oh, very. They're commonly pets, like the Nigerian Dwarf."

The van slows down as we approach a large farm-house. Behind it, an expansive barn is surrounded by fenced pens.

I turn to the driver. "I'll pay for you to wait while I get her settled. Then we can return to Manhattan."

The man taps his phone. "All right. I'll adjust the trip." He opens his door, but I stop him. "I've got it. Take a moment to relax after that drive."

"You sure?" He peers into the rear-view mirror at Lucy.

Maybe I shouldn't have said it, but I didn't want him noticing we brought a goat.

I tug on the sliding door. It takes a moment to figure out how to shift the seat forward to let Lucy out. I wish it were darker, so maybe the goat wouldn't be so obvious. Not that it matters. If he ditches me over it, I'll call another car.

But he's back on his phone, and he doesn't pay us much mind as we unload the goat, Lucy's knapsack, her new clothes, and the lunch coolers.

A woman appears from the barn, a bucket in her hands, and waves. "Bring that sweet girl over here!" she calls. I'm assuming she means the goat.

Lucy has found her people.

We walk in that direction. I cast a glance back at the van, but the driver is having an animated conversation with someone.

"Are you Lucy?" the woman asks.

"I am."

She fills a trough with her bucket, and the goats inside the pen come running. "You're gonna pop any day. When's your due date?"

"September 20."

"That's coming fast." The woman hangs the bucket on a nail and deftly hops over the fence. "I'm Caroline Halson. My husband Tom and I run the goat farm."

"Do you teach the yoga? I was an instructor in Colorado until I got too far along."

"Did you really? No, I'm not much into yoga myself.

But we have two instructors who take turns teaching our goat yoga. It's great fun. You can come to any class you like while you're staying."

"That's wonderful. Where should Matilda go? She hasn't been in a herd since I got her shortly after she kidded about a year ago."

"We can test her out with the pygmies, see how it goes."

I watch all this with fascination. The two of them look a lot alike, tall and easy with their movements, hair flying, no fuss about their appearance. Caroline is older than her, late forties, but I can see a lot about the two of them in common. It's in how they carry themselves, their love for the animals, the way their eyes alight on their surroundings. They're in their element.

I am not. My shiny leather Burberry dress shoes are already caked with mud. My pant cuffs are damp. I stand stiffly, hands clasped behind me, uncomfortable with the green coolers hanging from my shoulder, and the Naturalist Outfitters bag dangling from my fingers.

"Is this your husband?" Caroline asks. "I only saw you and Matilda on the reservation."

"Oh, no," Lucy says. "He's handling the accommodations for me."

Caroline reaches down to stroke Lucy's goat. "You rented the place for a month. Do you intend to have the baby while you're here?"

Lucy hesitates, looking at me.

I take a step forward, almost skidding in the damp earth. "We'll be looking for an obstetrician in the area. She'll be taken care of."

Caroline's eyebrows furrow. "And you are?"

I extend a hand. "Court Armstrong. I'm helping Lucy as she prepares for her baby."

Caroline shakes it uncertainly. "Well, all right. We have a good hospital about fifteen minutes away."

Lucy glances at me. "Perfect, thank you."

"Come this way. I'll show you the tiny house." She walks ahead of us. "It'll be quiet this weekend and during the week, but next weekend, we're fully booked with the farm expo happening so close. Let me know if you'd like to go. It's fun."

"I might!" Lucy follows, patting her leg so that her goat will go with her.

Our unusual party arrives at a semi-circle of tiny houses, each with its own small fenced yard.

Caroline opens the gate. "If Matilda doesn't take to the herd, you can keep her in the yard. We don't allow them in the houses, though. Will that be all right?"

"I can sleep outside with her if she gets upset," Lucy says.

I'm about to protest this, but Caroline gets there first. "There's an extra cot folded up beneath your bed. We can set that up. I bet she'll like the barn."

Really? She's encouraging a pregnant woman to sleep outside? But what do I know? Lucy's yurt barely qualifies as indoors.

When we're all inside the fence, Lucy bends down to take the diaper off the goat. "You're free!" she says.

"Poop at will," Caroline says, and they both laugh.

What kind of world is this? Not mine, that's for sure.

Caroline unlocks the front door. "It's small but tidy and homelike." She steps aside.

Lucy goes in. The goat tries to follow, but Caroline reroutes the goat to a shrubbery by the door.

I follow Lucy inside with the bags. There's a tiny kitchen, and beyond it, a space with a sofa on one side and a table on the other. At the back is a small bedroom and a bathroom.

"I love it," Lucy says. She sets her knapsack on the sofa.

I leave the coolers and bag on the table. "You all set?"

She nods. "Thank you. This place is perfect."

"Good." I rock back on my heels, not sure what to say next.

She runs her hands on her skirt, like she's sweaty. Nervous, maybe? "I'll let you know when the phone arrives. And when I have a doctor appointment."

"Good, good."

We stand there a moment, looking at each other.

She extends a hand. "Thank you, Court."

It feels strange to shake it after this wild, unexpected day. "We'll be in touch."

I don't look back as I head out the front door, past Caroline and the goat chomping on the leaves of the shrub.

I almost skid in the mud again but make it back to the van in one piece.

"Ready?" the driver says.

"Yes. Thank you."

He backs up to the narrow lane.

I've gotten through the first phase of this strange new world. It feels like a year since Lucy showed up in my office, barefoot and pregnant.

But it's only been one day.

There are miles to go in this conundrum before I see it through.

A month at least.

And maybe, a whole lot more.

# 11

## LUCY

B y the time I've put away the food and my meager things, I'm shot. Thankfully, Caroline is well versed in introducing a new goat to a herd. She returns and reports that Matilda is settled in perfectly.

I'm relieved and fall asleep the moment my head hits the pillow, curled up in the big T-shirt Court got me.

I wake up to the wonderful sounds of *meh eh eh* and the unique ring of grain being poured into a metal trough.

I get up, eat some of my leftovers, and put on the first new outfit since I left Colorado, the yellow sundress.

I find some duct tape in a drawer and mend my old shoes since I'll probably get muddy. I don't want to ruin my new ones.

The day is bright and warm. Some of the goats approach me as I walk out. Others are kept in the pens.

I reach down to pet their heads. "You must be the good goats."

A man in his early fifties waves from the barn. "You must be Lucy!"

I head over. "Is Matilda in there with you?"

"She sure is! She's a sweetheart!" He walks over to the gate and swings it open for me.

I spot Matilda standing on a rough-hewn wood platform. There are several of them scattered around for this purpose. Other goats have taken up the rest.

"She's been chill, just observing." The man extends a hand. "I'm Tom, Caroline's husband. Glad to have you."

When Matilda spots me, she jumps down and dashes over in her funny, loping gait. I pet her head. "This is a wonderful farm."

"We have lots of goats," Tom says. "Goat yoga will be starting soon, so the ones that participate in that will be heading to their duties. The rest stay inside the pen. You going to do it?"

"I'm going to rest another day before jumping into exercise," I say, running my hand over my belly as if it isn't wildly obvious.

"Caroline said you were about a month out. And a yoga teacher?"

"I have been. Looking forward to being able to do a forward fold without looking like a nutcracker."

Tom laughs. "Now that's a picture. Feel free to wander around."

And I do, putting Matilda on a lead in case she gets startled. I don't want her taking off in an unfamiliar place.

We have a pleasant walk through the front grounds.

It's filled with trees, and the barn is well kept. The lane down the middle keeps going into a more heavily forested area in the back, but we don't walk far.

By the time I return, goat yoga is in full swing. I watch from outside the low white fence that marks the yoga yard. About ten women have spread out their mats, and six goats wander among them.

Cute. Caroline approaches from the main house, waving a small box. "I got a delivery for you while you were walking," she calls.

The phone. Court was quick.

I take it from her. "Thank you. I'll get you my number as soon as I figure out what it is."

"New phone?"

"Yes." I don't explain further. I like it here, and I don't want any strange feelings. "I'll need to milk Matilda. Is there a place for that?"

"Yes, there's a milking shed attached to the barn. Water. Buckets. Whatever you need."

"Perfect."

I leave Matilda in the barn to look over the phone. It's been years since I had one of my own. It takes some effort to relearn the swipes and pinches to make it work. I find Court's information and text him I have it.

Within a half hour, I've set up a new email account, searched the area for OB/GYNs, and made an appointment with a nurse practitioner since I could get in more quickly. I forward that to Court, who hasn't responded to my first message, and head out to milk Matilda.

This is the life. I sit with Matilda for a while after

we've filled three of the Dill with It bottles. Then I store the bottles in my fridge and take a nap.

Court doesn't get back to me until evening, with two quick responses.

*Glad the phone arrived.*

*Thank you for your appointment information.*

I run my finger over the screen. No indication of whether or not he might come. Just acknowledgment.

Even with his salty self, I miss seeing him. It was a strange, intense day in his office.

And now, I just have to wait for the baby to be born.

I have enough food for the weekend, and Matilda and I spend the days easily. I turn her milk into goat cheese and soap with the supplies I packed, but they won't last long.

Caroline sells her own products locally, and I don't want to compete with that. I locate the spa owner's card that Kaliyah gave me and email her to negotiate some sales.

Then I look up Stanley's Emporium, not sure if Stanley really wanted my goat cheese after meeting me on the subway, or if he was being nice. A woman takes my name and number and says he'll call me later.

I hesitate with the phone, considering whether I should contact April and Summer now that I can.

Maybe so.

I rummage through the bottom of my knapsack where I hide a few important things. My wallet with my driver's license, which I've kept active even though I haven't had a car in years. My meager cash. And a couple of sticky notes from the yoga studio with the phone numbers of important people.

This includes April, even though it's the middle of the night in France.

And Summer, on the new phone her boyfriend gave her right before they left to elope in Vegas.

*Me: New phone! It's Lucy!*

I get an instant reply from Summer.

*Summer: Did you have that baby yet?*

Me: Not for a few weeks.

*Summer: Are you still in the yurt?*

How to answer that? As I type, delete, and re-type, April pops in.

*April: I was about to go to bed! Lucy! You're on the grid!*

*Me: I got a phone from Court. From New Year's.*

*April: What!*

*Summer: You called him?*

*Me: I'm in New York. He found a farm for me and Matilda to live on until the baby is born.*

*April: He did what!*

*Summer: Are you happy there? Did you have sex with him again? ARE YOU GETTING MARRIED?*

I wait until their barrage of questions dies down.

*Me: No proposal. I'm here until the paternity test.*

*April: How long?*

*Summer: Asshat!*

I go with April's comment.

*Me: We'll swab the baby's cheek when he's born.*

They continue to pepper me with questions long into the night, until they seem content they know everything.

It's good to have friends again. I plug the phone into the wall before I go to sleep, such a simple thing I've not done in a long time.

On Monday, I get an advance of money from the spa for soap and can breathe easier. I take an Uber to a grocery store and carefully pick out a few things I can afford, plus supplies to make more soap.

I'm making my way, little by little.

By the time the appointment rolls around on Thursday, I'm nervous again. Will Court show up? I'm really hoping so.

I Uber to a small community clinic within sight of the bigger hospital complex. The petite woman with glossy black hair asks questions about my prenatal history. "We'll probably repeat a few things since we don't have complete records. Bloodwork. Then fit you in for a sonogram. Gina will also do a quick glance at your cervix, since you're new and so close. Is that all right?"

I nod, watching the door.

She smiles. "Is Dad late?"

I don't know what to say to that. "He works in Manhattan. It's not easy for him to come."

She nods.

I almost ask about the paternity test but decide against it. I'm not doing an amnio, and the hospital will be the time to swab the baby. I can bring it up then.

"Gina will be in soon," the nurse says. "Go ahead and undress all the way, gown open to the front."

"Okay." When she leaves, I turn to the neatly stacked gown and paper cover on a small bench in the back corner.

I hate this part, always feeling like I'm racing to change before someone might come in.

My belly hinders me a hundred ways as I slip out of the new shoes and pull the yellow dress over my head. I got a maternity bra at a thrift store before I left Colorado, but it has far more hooks than my old ones. It takes more bendiness than I currently possess to reach them all. So much for all that yoga. I'm losing my flexibility.

Lightning pains dart through me as I reach. Seriously?

I'll have to do it another way. I pull my arms out of the straps and turn the bra to move the hooks to the front.

I'm tussling with it when the door opens without a knock.

No! My worst nightmare!

But it gets worse.

As I turn, standing in nothing but panties, my belly as big as the moon, my boobs hanging out over the back of the still-hooked bra, the person standing in the doorway isn't the nurse. Or Gina, the PA.

It's Court Armstrong.

## 12

## COURT

T his is an unexpected sight.

Lucy halts in whatever she was doing, nearly every inch of her glowing, smooth skin on display as she changes.

Her long, toned legs lead to the round belly, topped by breasts that are wholly different from the ones I encountered in Colorado eight months ago.

They're soft and full, tipped in rosy nipples that have already brought about a reaction in my groin.

She's fighting a bra that she probably can't see beneath that ample chest. Do I stay or go?

I've already seen everything. She looks like she needs help.

I quickly click the door closed. "Are you okay?"

She doesn't say anything, just turns around. The bra comes off, and my groin tightens further. Her fingers lock on her panties, and I'm frozen in place, unable to take my eyes off her.

"Can you please turn around?" she asks. "I'm big and bloated, and this is too much."

"But you're beautiful," I stammer, then frown at my discomposure. I shouldn't say those things. That's not who we are.

"Right. Stretch marks and all." She picks up the gown and drags it on, and only when she's covered, does she step out of the panties.

I'm staring. I force myself to turn my back to her and examine a poster illustrating how an infant's head descends through the birth canal. That cools my jets.

Lucy glides past me to the exam table, unfolding a paper sheet.

A change of subject might be best. "How is the goat farm?"

Her whole face lights up. "It's wonderful. Matilda and I watch the goat yoga. I've been making soap for the spa we went to. They paid me in advance, so I have money for groceries."

"Oh. Food." I should have thought of that. She'll need money for other things. "Should I provide an account for you?"

"You're doing more than enough. I'll manage."

"I can't have you going hungry."

"Oh, I won't. I'm pretty resourceful."

"Even so. There are probably certain foods you should be eating. Vitamins, perhaps?"

A knock at the door interrupts. A mid-forties woman with two puffs of black hair peeks in. "Hello! I'm Gina!"

I step aside as she enters.

"I hear we're having a baby!" She sets an iPad down on the counter. "It's so nice to meet you both."

"I'm Lucy." Lucy extends a hand. "Sorry to drop a late-term pregnancy on you."

"Happens all the time. People move. Get new jobs. We haven't been able to access your old records yet, but hopefully, they'll catch up." She turns to Court. "Who do we have here?"

I like that she doesn't assume I'm the father. "I'm Court." I shake her hand.

"This is a delight. Let's meet baby!" She helps Lucy lie back on the exam table.

"Let's see where the baby's lying." Gina separates the gown and presses both hands around the edges of Lucy's belly. "Have you had any troubles so far?"

"Just the tendon pains."

Gina nods and keeps feeling. "Tell me about those."

"I was teaching yoga until a couple of weeks ago. But I started getting darting pains and kept having to stop."

"And you saw your doctor?"

"I did. They were thorough, but there was only the tendon issue left."

"It's very common. The place where the ligament connects to the muscle gets stretched to its limit near the end. If you rest, does it resolve?"

"Yes."

Gina picks up Lucy's wrist. I'm fascinated by everything.

"I'm going to take a listen and do some measurements. Then a quick cervix check, nothing too invasive."

The room goes quiet as Gina looks at her watch, holding Lucy's wrist. "Your heart rate is 82, which is fine. And now I'll know which is yours and which is the baby's. Do you know the gender?"

"It's a boy."

I almost interject that she's only done a test with a string, but Gina says, "Good. The sonogram will confirm it if it wasn't perfectly clear before."

"Oh, I'm clear," Lucy says.

"Mothers often know." Gina folds the paper sheet down. "Baby is in the proper head down position, and everything feels perfect. Let's listen to that heart."

She squirts clear gel on the end of a probe the size of a small flashlight. "We'll go for baby first, but we might get Mom."

When she flicks on the power, a static sound fills the room, like an old television set on an empty channel. But when she presses it to the side of Lucy's belly, there's an immediate rapid whomp, whomp sound that eradicates the static.

"There it is," Gina says. "One-fifty, perfect heart rate." She turns to me. "Do you hear that?"

"It never gets old," Lucy says.

I shouldn't feel anything. This child could belong to anyone. But Lucy's dreamy smile, Gina's happy grin, and the proof of the life beating inside her do something to me.

A rush of emotion rises from my belly, stinging my eyes and nose. I clamp it down. It doesn't suit me. This baby could be anyone's.

Gina turns to me. "You should record it with your

phone for her. Patients like to listen to it when they're anxious. It's soothing."

Relieved to have something to do, I tug my phone from my pocket and slide it to video. The focus stays on the probe, Lucy's smiling face mildly blurred in the background. The sound reverberates, *whomp, whomp, whomp.*

"That's your son," Lucy says, her voice catching. She isn't saying it like a woman on a talk show who's trying to snag a baby daddy. There is no insistence, no question. She says it simply, like you might point out, "That's my mom." Or, "Come meet my sister."

My throat tightens. Our gazes meet, and another wave crashes over me. Damn it. I flip off the phone and shove it back in my pocket.

"We'll listen to Mom for a second, make sure blood flow is good to the baby." Gina moves the probe and after a moment, a slower, heavier beat takes over the sound.

"Eighty-two, right on the money. Sounds perfect." Gina switches off the machine and uses a white towel to wipe the gel off Lucy's belly. "I'm going to do a quick feel of the cervix to make sure there are no surprises, then I'll send you to schedule your follow-ups."

My phone beeps, and it's a blessed distraction. I turn away to look at the text. It's nothing, just a reminder of a meeting uptown at three, but I use it as an excuse to punch nonsense into my phone like I must reply.

"That's it!" Gina says.

There's a rustle, and I turn to see Gina helping Lucy sit up. "You look perfect. Let me know if those pains get more intense, or you feel like it's contractions instead. I'd like to see you every week until you deliver. Make sure to schedule a sonogram before you leave, and they'll give you paperwork for the bloodwork at checkout."

Lucy nods. She steps down, pulling the gown around her. "I'll make the appointments."

"So nice to meet you both. We'll bring Dr. Henry in on your next visit so you can meet him. He'll be the one called in when you deliver."

"Will you be there?" Lucy asks. "Everyone is so new."

"I make rounds too, but Dr. Henry will perform the winning catch!"

It's meant to be a funny statement, but something in Lucy breaks, and there goes the tears again.

Gina looks at me. When I don't move, she opens her arms, and Lucy steps in for a hug.

This is unexpected. Gina holds onto her for a long moment as Lucy weeps into her shoulder. Gina looks over her at me. "Pregnancy is an emotional time. You go and snuggle up to this strong man of yours and cry all you need to."

She turns Lucy to me. I'm not sure what to do but accept her in my arms.

"There you go," Gina says. "You two are going to be fine. Call if you need anything."

I plan to release Lucy as soon as Gina closes the door, but Lucy doesn't let go, crying softly on my shoulder. So I leave my arms around her. I admit it must be hard for her, surrounded by strangers, in a city where she knows no one, having a baby.

Her body heaves with each breath, like it's a great difficulty.

What am I supposed to do with this? I barely know her.

But I stay there, simply holding onto her until she seems spent.

"I'm fine," she says.

Right. Crying for five minutes straight is fine.

"We should have asked Gina about the DNA test."

I realize it's an asshole thing to say the minute it's out. But it's done.

Lucy lets out a long breath. "Can we wait until the hospital for that? It's hard enough showing up at a new clinic this late term."

"All right. We can't do it until then, anyway."

She moves to the corner where her clothes are. "Will you turn away this time?" Her voice is dull and sad.

I'm sure I did that to her. This is why no one should pin their happiness on me. I'm not up for the job.

In fact, this kid, even if he is mine, should probably stay far away.

If I can be raised by two perfectly good parents in a normal, happy family, and turn out like this, then there's no hope for something as gentle and impressionable as a small child, not around me.

## 13

## LUCY

I can't read Court's mood at all. He's swinging faster than a carnival ride.

I thought for a moment, when we were listening to the baby's heartbeat, that he felt something. He got so still. So fully attentive.

But then he was back to his usual self, barely letting me dress without bringing up paternity.

He doesn't believe the baby is his. And if he doesn't, he can't bond with his child.

At least not until the paternity test is done.

We check out, and I schedule bloodwork and a sonogram for next week. Court is impassive, giving me only the smallest nod when the clerk tells me what times are available.

This is going worse than I hoped.

As we walk out, he says, "I can take you back to the farm. I brought my car."

That's something, I guess. I'm emotional from the doctor visit and want to make progress, anything I can get, in forging some sort of partnership for when the baby is born. He may not believe it's his, but I *know*.

The sunlight is blinding, and I shield my eyes as Court unlocks a sleek black Ferrari, low to the ground, and wildly sexy. It's definitely a fit for him.

He almost sits behind the wheel, then realizes he should probably be polite, and rounds the car to open the passenger side.

I peer down at the low-slung seat with trepidation. I'm not sure I can get in, much less get out.

I duck my head and hang onto the edge of the door as I maneuver inside. There's nothing for my left hand to grab onto. The dash is too far forward. The steering wheel is out of reach.

I hesitate, worried I'm about to fall onto the seat in a heap of yellow dress and belly.

"Everything okay?" Court asks.

I back out. "Trying to figure out how to sit down."

He leans down to peer inside. "I guess it is a little low."

"I'll figure it out."

I try putting a leg in first, but I can't get my butt anywhere near the seat. I'm afraid to let go of the door. I don't want to fall into place. It feels like a mile between my body and the seat.

I hover over the cushion, but my arm starts to shake. I'm about to crash land when Court leans down and cradles my thighs and back.

"Here you go," he says, lowering me carefully.

As I expected, the seat is too deep for me to sit properly, so I have to stretch out to fit. I can't bend in half enough to settle onto the bottom.

"Maybe if we lower the back." Court reaches for a lever, and the rear cushion hums as it smoothly lies back.

His face is perilously near mine as I settle more comfortably on the seat. As I slide down and below him, it's almost the same feeling as falling onto a bed. I flash with the one night we knew each other, his face hovering over mine.

And there it is, that intense flash of need. I suck in a breath.

His palm flies to my belly. "The pains?"

"No. I'm fine."

He lifts his hand away like he got burned. "This position seems better. Is it?"

"It's good."

His gaze meets mine for a split second, and I almost wonder if he's remembering New Year's Eve as well.

Then he pulls back and tugs the seatbelt down. He starts to stretch it over my belly, but I take it from him. "I've got it."

My hand brushes his as I take the latch. Fire licks through me. Stupid pregnancy hormones. What's the point? I'm already reproducing! There's absolutely no point to having him in me.

And yet, as he closes the door and walks around the back of the car, I flap my hand at my overheated face. All I can think about is his body over mine, sliding into me, my hands clutching his shoulders.

Now I'm the one swinging. Tears. Anger. Lust.

"You sure you're okay?" He's in his seat, pulling on his own belt, and I still haven't latched mine.

I shove it into place. "I'm good. Gina was nice, right?"

"I think we should have seen the doctor."

"Next time. It was short notice."

Court grunts as he reverses out of the lot.

We're back at the farm in mere minutes. I want to ask him to come in. To eat lunch. For us to talk.

But I can't find the words.

"Do you need me for the bloodwork?" he asks.

"No, of course not."

"You don't faint?"

"No, I'm pretty hearty that way."

He nods. "All right. Then I'll see you afterward at the sonogram. Are you taking a birthing class?"

"I already did, with my friends. They like you to do it in the second trimester."

"I see."

I should have lied, asked him to do one with me. Damn it. I have to think on my feet a little better.

He pulls up to the fence in front of my tiny house.

I unlatch the belt but immediately struggle to sit up in the seat.

"Hold on." Court jumps out and comes around.

Then his head is over mine again, and he's helping me roll to my side so I can push up and out of the car.

"I'll bring something more appropriate next time," he says.

"You have more than one car?"

"I can rent something."

It's a relief to be standing again. "Thank you for coming."

He closes the door. "No problem."

"Did you have to cancel meetings?"

"I can move things around." His face is grim. "I'm the boss."

I wait by the gate as he gets into this car and backs out of the drive. I stand there long after his gleaming black car disappears down the lane.

He's something.

The goats roam the big pen, and I spot Matilda by herself in the corner. Poor girl. She's not used to so many roommates.

I hurry inside to grab her lead and spring her from the pen. It's late morning but not too hot yet. We walk along the backlot, taking the dirt road that leads into the trees. She'll enjoy foraging for brush.

It's the farthest we've gone since arriving, but I'm feeling good knowing the baby is okay, and Court will be coming to the visits.

"I saw Court today," I tell Matilda. "He was less salty than usual for a hot second when he heard the heartbeat."

Matilda pauses to chew on a shrub. She doesn't hold up her end of a conversation, that's for sure.

I spin a fantasy while I wait for her to move on. Court and I outside a little house with a fence for Matilda, the baby running in the yard. We sit side by side on a porch swing, a gentle breeze ruffling our hair.

He puts his arm around me. And I'm content. Absolutely happy.

Matilda nudges my knee.

"Hey, girl." We keep walking through the copse of trees until I hear the rumble of a motor behind me. We have to step aside as a refrigerated truck passes us on the road. The side of it is emblazoned with dancing cartoon steaks and the words "McKenzie Meats."

What is that doing here?

I quicken my step to follow it until we hit a clearing. A sign here announces, "Halson Goat." The driver unloads an empty cart and pushes it toward the side door of a long, sleek barn.

I glance back up the lane. The Halson family goat-milk operation is all housed in the front barn. What is this?

The smell is strong back here. I can hear the bleats of many, many goats.

At first, Matilda walks alongside me, but once we get closer, she halts in her tracks.

I have to pull and coax her into moving forward. At first, everything seems fine. More fencing, a huge pasture, and plenty of space beyond. Dozens of goats roam the wide pen.

These goats are males. I can tell by the smell. Probably they're put here after kidding since only the females can produce milk.

But why so many? They far outnumber the milk goats up front.

The door opens again, and the delivery man wheels his cart out, stacked with boxes.

My heart hammers. He's taking boxes from the property to his refrigerated meat truck?

I move closer. There's print on the side of the box, an arc of words over an illustration of a goat.

Halson Family Farm Goat Meat.

Meat.

Of goat.

I feel faint.

A door squeaks at the end of the barn. I expect to see hay bales and dirt floor, but it's not. It's pristine white and silver.

With rows of hanging goat carcasses.

I stumble backwards. The males have spotted Matilda and move toward the fence.

All these goats. Just waiting to be taken inside and hung on those hooks.

I don't care about the pain in my belly. I whirl around and take off in as fast a run as I can manage, pulling Matilda with me. The delivery truck catches up to us, but I'm not on the road, so it roars past.

We don't stop until we're in my tiny house. I bring Matilda with me. I don't care that she's not supposed to be here. They can kick me out.

I'm leaving anyway.

I can't be here another minute.

Not with that happening so close by.

Those goats!

Those poor sweet goats!

I throw everything in my knapsack and carefully pack my goat milk and soap in the coolers, dumping ice from the freezer around the containers.

I haul everything onto my shoulders and race out the door, walking up the lane as fast as I can.

People arrive for noontime goat yoga, parking their cars along the fence.

"They kill goats here!" I cry, walking swiftly to the road. "They butcher them and wrap them in plastic and sell them!"

Some of the women look at me curiously.

My belly hurts, and I bend over a moment to manage the pain.

Then I keep going, past the cars, down the long drive.

I realize when I reach the main road that I should have already called an Uber Pet. I pull out my phone, trembling with misery and rage. I try to punch the buttons to book the Uber, but what if they turn me down? Matilda isn't even wearing her diaper.

Matilda trots away from the road, startled by a car. I drop my bags, trying to hang onto her lead. I manage to find the Uber Pet, but there's nothing available to book for hours.

I sit in the grass as the cars whiz by. What do I do? Where do I go?

I can't go back there. I just can't.

There's no subway out here.

The sun shines down, bright and unrelenting. Sweat beads on my forehead. I can't stay out here long. I'll pass out from the heat. I should have drunk some water before leaving.

I can think of nothing else to do.

So I call Court.

## 14

## COURT

I haven't even reached the Lincoln tunnel when I get a call from Lucy. I hear her heavy sob-laden breathing before she even talks.

"Lucy, are you okay?"

"Come get me." Her voice is high and squeaky. "Please come back and get me."

I signal to change lanes so I can turn around. "What's going on?"

"They killed the goats. They sell them!"

Jesus. Did they do something to her goat?

"When?"

"Just now. I saw a meat truck, and I saw them hanging from hooks." The last word dissolves into a sob.

"Did they mix up your goat?"

"Matilda? No. She's here with me."

I let out a sigh of relief. That would have been the worst. "So you saw the dead goats?"

"Those poor babies! They strung them up, like meat!"

I decide not to point out that the goats are, in fact, meat. Devin clearly didn't check into this farm well enough. I had no idea there was a butchery operation out there as well. But it was a lot of land. I should have known there was more to it.

"Where are you?" I ask her.

"By the Goat Yoga sign."

"Where they do the yoga in the yard?" It's pushing ninety degrees. She should go inside.

"No, the one by the main road."

"Lucy! That's not safe. Get away from the road."

"I can't go back there."

I grip the steering wheel hard. "It's not safe for you or the baby or the goat to be that close to traffic. Please back away. Get in some shade at least."

I hear a rustling sound.

"Are you moving?"

"There's a tree by the fence."

I glance at the clock. I left her forty-five minutes ago. I'll try to make it back in thirty. "Just sit tight, Lucy. I'll be there."

"Okay."

"If you get thirsty, please go back to your tiny house and get a drink. You can't see the—" What do I even call it? "The other goats from there, right?"

"No. They were down a dirt road I hadn't been on before."

"Please tell me you'll head back if you feel sick or hot."

"Okay."

She ends the call. Damn it. I put through a call to Devin.

"Yeah, boss. You about back? Your next meeting is in a half hour."

"Cancel it. I'm returning to Warwick."

"Something wrong with Lucy?"

"Did you know they sold goat meat on the property? They raise the goats and do the butchering?"

"I did not."

I can hear him tapping. I dodge in and out of traffic to push the limit of how fast I can get back to her.

Devin says, "There's no mention of this anywhere on their site, but now that I have specifically looked for it, I do see that they sell goat meat wholesale from another building. It's a good quarter-mile back on the property on the other side of a forest. She found it?"

"Apparently so."

"Poor thing. That must have been hard on someone with her sensibilities."

"She's sitting by the side of the road, waiting for me to get her."

"You're going to put the goat in your Ferrari?"

Right. I glance in the back. Will it even fit back there? Plus, this car had been hard for Lucy to ride in. And she hadn't even complained about the leather seats.

"What can I rent between here and Warwick?"

More tapping. "I see three car rental places."

"Call them. Get me an SUV with the keys in it, ready to go. I'll park the Ferrari in their lot until I can come back for it."

"I can make that happen."

He better.

I pass a semi to gain some ground. "Let me know when you have it booked. No leather seats if you can help it."

"Roger that."

I weave between lanes, roaring past anyone who slows me down. By the time I'm approaching Warwick, Devin has dropped a pin where the car is.

Good man.

Five minutes later, I've parked my Ferrari in a lot and switched to a sporty SUV. This is better. I only lost three minutes on this maneuver but gained a lot of space and probably saved my Ferrari.

This one has cloth seats and an artic-level air conditioner. I crank it, knowing I'll need to cool her down. As I approach the goat farm, I see Lucy in her yellow dress, sitting in the grass under a tree, her goat eating leaves off a bush.

I pull over onto the shoulder and shove the car into park.

It takes her a second to realize it's me. She stands, shielding her eyes.

I wait for traffic to pass, then jump out and hurry to her.

"What's this car?" she asks. Her cheeks are flush, and her arm, as I pull her up, is hot to the touch.

"A rental so we could fit the goat."

"Her name is Matilda."

"Right, right." I help her to the car and open the passenger door. "You sit in the AC. I'll load the goat into the back."

"No, no, I'll sit in the backseat with her."

I meant the cargo bay, but I'm not going to argue. I open the rear door, and Lucy pats the seat. The goat jumps up, and Lucy follows. I pile her bags into the front seat and make sure plenty of air is flowing to her.

"This is better," she says.

I get behind the wheel, and for the first time since she called me, I realize I have no idea what I'm going to do with her.

This is a dilemma. As I signal and merge back onto the road, I try to figure out a solution. We have to vet any goat farms, or farms in general, before we choose another place.

I glance in the rear-view mirror. Lucy rests her head on her goat, weeping into her fur.

"Have you eaten lunch?" I ask her.

"I don't think I could."

"Let's at least stop and pick something up."

She doesn't respond.

At the next light, I search my phone for something suitable with a drive-thru. I find a sandwich shop with an extensive vegetarian menu and smoothies. I want something cold and caloric in her. She looks both pink and pale at the same time, wisps of hair curling around her temples.

When we pull up to the microphone to order, she says, "Can you ask for loose lettuce or carrots for Matilda?"

This will be fun. "Sure. What do you want?"

"Maybe a strawberry smoothie."

Perfect.

A woman's voice comes over the speaker. "May I take your order?"

"Yes, I need a large strawberry smoothie." I'll get some food, anyway. She might eat it later. "And a hummus and avocado on wheat. A cream cheese with sprouts on sourdough. And can I get a pile of lettuce on the side?"

There's silence for a minute, then the woman says, "What was that?"

"A pile of loose lettuce."

"Just lettuce? Nothing else."

"It's for a goat."

Silence.

"Did you get that?" I work to control the anger in my voice as heat rises from my gut.

"Oh, I got it. Strawberry smoothie. Hummus and avocado on wheat. Cream cheese and sprouts on sourdough. And lettuce for your goat."

"That's right." I catch Lucy watching out the window as if she can see the woman taking the order.

"Clarice, what do I charge for random lettuce?" the woman calls.

Another voice says, "What do you mean, random lettuce?"

She must realize her mic is on, because the speaker goes quiet.

"You'd think I asked for poop on a platter," Lucy says.

I force myself to hold back my laugh. "You'd think."

Finally, the speaker squawks again, "Twenty-three seventy-five. Pull up."

When I arrive at the window, I pass the woman a credit card. She gives me a plastic bag full of loose lettuce and peers into the car. "Clarice, there sure is a goat in there!"

Several other faces appear in the glass.

Lucy rolls down her window. "Her name is Matilda! She loves lettuce! It's like a cookie to her."

"It's like a cookie!" one of them repeats, as if it's the wildest thing they ever heard.

I hand Lucy the bag of lettuce and watch in the rearview as she feeds a leaf of it to the goat.

"Look at her chomping it!" one of the women cries. They all lift their phones to record it. Great. Hopefully, they keep me out of it. Axel and Rhett will never let me live this down if it goes viral.

Another car pulls up behind us, but nobody pays any attention as they video the goat. Finally, the other driver honks.

"Oh, hush, *Karen*," the woman says, but she runs my card through her reader and passes it back.

Eventually, we get our smoothie and sandwiches, and everyone waves and shouts, "Bye, Matilda the goat!" as I pull away.

Lucy sips her drink as the goat shoves her face into the lettuce bag. "That lifted my spirits. Thank you."

I pass her the sandwiches. "I thought you might get hungry once you cooled off."

"I'm starving. You're good at this." She unwraps one and takes a big bite.

"Good at what?" I glance at her reflection as I wait for a chance to pull out. Traffic is heavy.

"Taking care of a pregnant stranger."

"Oh, I've done it before. Twice actually."

"You have?" Her voice is incredulous. Then she smacks the back of my seat, choking with laughter. "It's a joke! You can be funny! See, I never knew that about you!"

"Don't get used to it." There's finally an opening, so I pull out.

Lucy shakes her head, merriment in her eyes. I can't stop glancing between the road and the sight of her behind me. "Court Armstrong, there's a lot more to you than meets the eye."

Maybe there used to be. To be honest, it feels strange to laugh or smile.

It's been a long, long time.

## 15

### LUCY

I expect Court to take me back to his office, but instead we pull up to a stone building with a canopy in front of big wood doors.

"Where are we?" I ask.

"My apartment building." He waits for a man in a maroon uniform to approach from the door.

"Oh, wait, I forgot about the goat." He guns the motor and takes off, leaving the uniformed man confused, his arms out.

"What just happened?"

"Normally, I leave my car with Jerry, the valet for the building. But we're not allowed pets without an addendum to our lease."

"How long will that take?"

"For a goat? A day past never."

We whip into a garage, and I clutch the door with one hand and Matilda with the other. We're plunged into near-dark until my eyes adjust.

"What are we doing?" I ask.

The side of Court's face that I can see is grim. "Apparently, we're going to sneak a goat up the stairs."

"This sounds fun!"

"A real lark." His tone is ominous, all joking gone. This is the Court I know.

"What happens if you get caught?"

"They'll probably throw me out."

"They can do that?"

"For a goat? Maybe. A dog, they'd fine me. But livestock is another matter entirely."

"Matilda isn't livestock!"

He grunts at that. We make a tight turn as we go higher in the garage.

We keep going up. The cars are shiny and new. They look unused. And do they all leave them with Jerry? I can't imagine handing over the keys to my car. What if you wanted to take off in the middle of the night? Would Jerry be there waiting?

But I don't ask. I hold on to Matilda as we make our way up.

We must be near the top. The ramp continues into open sky, but Court doesn't go up there. He parks the SUV near a door in the corner.

"I should probably bring the goat up the stairs. You can take the elevator."

That'll never work. "Matilda won't go with you."

"Why not?"

How to put this kindly? "She likes to butt you with her head."

"Right. But it's a lot of stairs. Ten floors, easily."

"Really? We drove forever."

"And the garage is much shorter than the tower."

Oh. I sit up tall. "I can do it. We can go slow."

"I'd feel better if you took the elevator." He pulls out his wallet and passes me a plastic card. "This is the key card for it."

I take it, but I'm skeptical. "She won't do it."

"I can handle a goat."

I'm not sure which one of them is more stubborn. "All right," I say. "Give it a go."

I open my door and tug Matilda out of the car. The moment her hooves are on solid ground, she poops everywhere. "Sorry," I tell Court.

"Better here than the car. We'll take care of it later."

"It's great for plants. Do you have any plants?"

"We're not putting goat poop in my plants."

"But you have some?" That sounds promising. Maybe there's a rooftop garden like I've seen in movies.

"No."

"Oh."

"I'll come back for your bags once we've made it up." He closes the door softly, like we're trying not to wake the neighbors.

I do the same with mine. "Should we whisper?"

"No. Of course not."

A car approaches from below, and Court jumps into action. He grabs the leash from me and drags Matilda to the front of the car.

She doesn't want to go and stiffens her legs.

Oh, no.

I turn and spread my skirt so the driver can't see her.

The man behind the wheel passes by without a glance our way. He takes the ramp up to the roof.

When I lower my skirt, I realize I've stepped in the goat poop.

"Oh, dear." I reach down and remove the shoes. I'm barefoot again.

"Just leave them there," Court hisses. "I'll take care of it when I come back down."

"But they're my new ones!"

"I'll take care of it!" His usually perfect hair falls in his eyes as he pulls on Matilda.

She won't budge.

"How to you get her to move?"

I set my soiled shoes by the front tire. "You catch more flies with honey."

"What are you talking about?"

I circle Matilda so I'm near her face. "You have to be nice, not mean." I croon in a sing-song. "Let's go, sweet pea. Mama wants to go inside."

The goat stares at Court, but I manage to rub her cheeks until she relaxes. "Let's go, Matilda."

She takes a step forward.

"Finally," Court says, yanking on the lead.

Matilda digs in again.

"I told you this wouldn't work," I tell Court.

"I'll pick her up. How much can she weigh?"

"I wouldn't—" But it's too late. Court has leaned down and shoved his arms under Matilda's belly.

Now, full grown Nigerian Dwarves tend to weigh around seventy-five pounds. Matilda is a little under that, around sixty-five last time I could get her on a scale.

But that is sixty-five pounds of pure ornery.

The minute her hooves are off the ground, she's bleating and squirming and kicking.

Court takes it on the thighs, then turns white in the face and lets go.

His knees fold together in a pose I'm not sure I've ever seen on a man.

I think she got him in the groin.

"Court? You okay?"

He leans against the car. "You're right. We'll all have to go." His voice is high and tight.

"You think we can make it to the elevator? Or is there someone always inside like in the movies?"

He shakes his head. "There's nobody in the elevator, but there is a camera."

"Oh, that won't do. They'll see her on security. What if we throw a blanket over her?"

He lifts his head at that. "That could work."

"I have the pickle one you got for me at your office." I open the driver's side and lean in to lift the flap of my knapsack. There's a lot of room since Matilda ate all the grain. I didn't restock at the farm because there was so much to eat there.

I'll have to get more again.

It might be a good thing Court doesn't have plants. Matilda would have them for snacks.

I tug out the Pickle blanket. "At least then they won't know she's a goat. If you get fined for a dog, I can save up and pay you back."

He lifts his hand. "It's okay."

I kneel in front of Matilda. "Okay, Matty, I'm going to cover you. You be a good girl, okay?"

I murmur at her as I unfold the blanket and lay it over her back. It's not bad. She looks more like a miniature pony now than anything.

"Let's give this a try," Court says, passing the leash to me. "God help us."

If we're looking for divine intervention, I'd rather divert it to the poor goats at the farm. I understand that people eat goats, just like they eat pigs and cows and chickens. But I don't want anything to do with it.

Court takes the plastic card from me and runs it across the lock on the door to the building. It pops open. "Let me scout," he says.

Matilda and I wait. The garage is warm with no breeze. "Be a good girl," I tell her.

She answers with a *meh eh eh*.

When Court returns, he tries to smooth his wild hair and tugs on his suit jacket to make it more presentable. I don't point out that it's covered in goat hair.

He holds the door open. "It's a long hall to the elevators, but this time of day should be quiet. Let's go."

He opens the door wide for me and Matilda to pass.

The halls are carpeted, like a hotel. Everything smells like fresh linen. "How do they get it to smell so good?" I ask.

"Fragrance in the air vents," he says. "Now come on."

He leads us past a door marked "Staff Only," and we turn right down a long hall. Each door is elegant, with a gold knocker and matching lever. Lamps on the wall give off a soft glow.

We creep along the hall with no trouble until we get to the elevator bank. Court presses the button, but when the doors slide open, there's a lady in a tall straw hat.

She stares at me, Court, and Matilda in the blanket, her mouth open, until the doors close again.

"Oh no," I say. "Are you busted?"

Court's eyes are wild. With his disheveled hair and rumpled, hairy suit jacket, he looks less corporate and more human. "I don't know."

He punches the up button again. It's an eternal wait, but the second elevator finally stops. This time, I'm careful to be out of view when it opens.

"It's empty," Court says.

We try to lead Matilda inside, but she doesn't like going into such a small enclosed space. She stiffens her legs.

"Good God," Court says. He picks up her hind legs, and before she can get a good kick in, he swings her around so she's half inside.

"I'm sorry, baby," I tell her, then shove her the rest of the way in.

The doors close.

Court punches the button for eighteen. It's not the top. There are twenty-six levels in the building. "Is there a penthouse?" I ask.

"Probably."

"But you don't live there."

"I'm not a billionaire in a romance novel," he says.

"I don't read romance novels."

"Why not?" He watches Matilda warily as the elevator rises.

"Books don't last very long in the yurt."

His gaze shifts to me. "The humidity?"

"Oh, no. Matilda loves to eat paper. It's just wood pulp."

"So Matilda might love romance novels."

Another joke! "Court, you are positively hilarious when you want to be."

The elevator slows to a stop. "Let me scout," Court says. "Hold the door open."

I can't quite reach the button with Matilda in the way and my belly so huge, so I stand in the door. Court steps out, looking each way.

"We're good. Let's go."

I pull on Matilda's lead, but she's dug in again. Apparently, she likes the elevator now.

The doors try to close, and I have to push on them to keep them apart. "Come on, Matilda," I cajole. "Follow Mommy."

She won't go. I tug and rub and talk to her. The elevator makes a terrible buzzing noise.

"It's been open too long," Court says. His face and neck have gone dark red.

"Should I go back in?"

"We have to get her out!"

"I have an idea," I say. "You won't like it."

"I don't exactly like this!"

I drop the lead. "Butt her head with your head, then run."

"What?"

"Butt her head. Be aggressive. She'll chase you then."

"Shit."

"She won't do it with me."

Court closes his eyes for a second. The elevator continues its horrible buzzing.

Then he bends over, head down, and rams Matilda in the nose.

"Run!" I say.

Court whips around and takes off down the hall.

Matilda gives chase, taking off like her life depends on it. The blanket falls to the floor.

I bend down with great difficulty to pick it up, then move out of the elevator. The doors close, and the terrible noise finally stops.

Matilda chases Court down the hall, and they disappear around a corner.

I guess I better try to catch up.

# 16

## COURT

W hen we're finally safely inside the apartment, I have to sit down.

I consider myself to be in good shape, but the mental wear and tear of the last two hours have been more than I'm used to.

Dashing back for Lucy, loading the goat. Unloading the goat. And the mad dash.

The rear of my pants feels weird against the cool leather cushion. I hop up and run my hands over the cloth.

"Yeah, Matilda got a good chomp on those." Lucy stands with her goat near the French doors to the balcony. "I like your boxers, though."

I look over my shoulder to spot a long swath of fabric hanging from my ass. What boxers did I put on today? Oh, right, the red silk ones. I'm sure they're quite the contrast.

"I'm going to change," I tell her.

"That's a leather sofa, isn't it?" Lucy asks.

"I didn't know you were coming."

"It's all right." She kneels behind it. "Thank you, sweet cow, for your sacrifice so that we might have furniture." She pets the back of the cushion as though she's comforting the long-dead bovine.

I shake my head and move on to my bedroom, phone in hand. I put through a call to Devin as I shuck my suit and put on workout shorts and a T-shirt.

"Everything okay, boss?" Devin asks.

"I won't be in today. Lucy is with me. We'll need to figure out a new situation for her."

"It will probably have to wait a few days."

"Why?"

"I started looking after I got the car. There's some farming event happening this weekend, and everything rural is booked for miles. We'd have to go three hours out of the way."

"When can you get her something? Monday?"

"Yes. Or Tuesday. I'm having to vet everything for anything that might upset her."

"Of course. Let me know what you find."

"You'll be in tomorrow for the Friday staff meeting?"

"I plan to. Text me if you need anything."

I drop the phone on my bed. Three days with a goat.

Speaking of which, I hear a plaintive *meh eh eh* from the other room, followed by, "Matilda, shhh! The neighbors!"

I hurry back down the hall. Lucy stands by the bookcase, where the goat is straining toward my collection of Bridgerton special editions.

"Don't let her eat those. They've gone out of print." I rush forward to move the books higher.

"You read romances?"

"Is that derision in your voice? Men can like romances."

She pulls on the goat. "You don't seem like the type."

"And what type is that?"

She grunts with the effort of keeping my romance collection safe. "Salty sons of bitches."

This makes me full-on laugh. "You cuss!"

"Matilda! Come on!" Lucy manages to get the goat to turn around. "The place isn't very goat proof."

"I wasn't exactly planning on having a goat here."

She blows hair out of her way. "Is there anywhere safe?"

"The balcony."

She nods.

"Let me get some greens." I rush to the kitchen and pull out an entire bag of carrots. I return to find Lucy with her arms around the goat, trying to keep her away from a shelf of classic records in their cardboard jackets.

"Don't let her eat those either!" I hold out the carrots.

The goat sniffs, then takes a tentative step in my direction.

"She loves carrots," Lucy says.

"You can have all the carrots you want," I say, waving them at her.

I lead her to the French doors and throw one open. I toss a carrot onto the ground.

But the goat isn't dumb. She knows I have more.

I hold out another and let her nibble on the end. Then I lead her through the door.

"Is there anything out there she can destroy?" Lucy asks.

"No, just metal furniture. I keep the cushions in an airtight box."

She's almost out. I toss the rest of the carrots onto the concrete floor. Just a little farther, then yes, her butt is out of the way, and I close and latch the door.

"Is it too hot for her out there?" Lucy asks.

I flip two switches, one for the overhead fan on the balcony, and another for a side fan with a built-in mister.

"Oh, that's lovely!" Lucy stands by the door as her goat preens in the thin spray. "We'll get her a spread of hay and some water, and she'll be all right." She turns, her face drawn and pale. "I think I should sit down."

"I have a spare room. Come on."

She doesn't move, holding onto the back of the sofa. She's fading completely.

"Okay, up you go." I pick her up—I swear I've carried her more than any woman in my life—and take her down the hall.

I lay her on the bed and turn on the overhead fan.

She curls onto her side and runs a hand over the blue and white French provincial bedspread. "It's so lovely in here."

"I'll get you some water."

"And some for Matilda."

"Some for her, too."

I fill a glass with filtered water and take it to her.

"Matilda?"

"Right." She really does care more for that goat than for herself.

I return to the kitchen to pull out a huge Dutch oven from a lower cabinet and fill it with water. The goat is ingesting carrots and pooping them out at a similar rate. I'll have to warn my housekeeper.

I open the door and slide the water out.

Then I return to Lucy. "All handled."

"Good." Her eyes flutter. "I'm sorry I'm so much trouble. She's all I have."

"No, you also have me."

She manages a smile. "I do. And you take good care of us."

I sit on the edge of the bed. "What should I get for you two?"

"Pellets for Matilda and some hay. Can you find that in the city?"

"I'll figure it out. And for you?"

"You have already done so much."

"It's fine. We're fine." I frown. "Are you sure you don't want to call your family?"

At that, a single tear escapes from the corner of her eye and slides to the bedspread. "Not yet. Not unless I have to."

There has to be more at play than environmental differences. It's probably a story for later. "Okay. You rest."

She nods, and I head for the door.

"Court?"

I turn around.

"I hope you believe me."

"About what?"

"The baby. I know you need proof, but there was nobody else. Not for a long time before. Not after. It can only be you."

"Okay, Lucy. I believe you."

"Good." Her eyes drift closed.

I run my hands through my hair as I walk my apartment, looking for critical things the goat could destroy and putting them away in closets.

When things are reasonably secure, I stand at the balcony to look at the goat. She seems to be asleep, standing stock still, her eyes closed. Water is sloshed out of the Dutch oven, and the carrots are gone.

I head back to the hall and do the same check at Lucy's doorway. She's curled around her belly, the yellow dress spread across the bed. Her feet are dirty again. That seems to be her status quo.

Time to arrange for the SUV's return and my car to come back. Then clean up the garage and fetch her things.

She's holding to her story about the baby. Maybe it's true. It's hard to believe I've gotten myself into a mess this huge.

Somehow, I've found myself in possession of three creatures who need me. A woman, a soon-to-be-baby, and a goat.

## 17

### LUCY

I wake Friday morning to voices.

Or maybe just one voice.

The clock reads eight a.m. I've slept through the afternoon and the night, and I'm not sure what bodily function is screaming the loudest—bladder, hunger, or thirst.

There's a bathroom attached to this room, blue and white to match the decor. I don't figure Court to be one to examine paint swatches, so I assume he used a decorator.

But then, I didn't expect him to have romance novels either.

It's a great relief to empty my bladder. As I wash up, I smooth down my wild hair. I need to check on Matilda before I do anything else, so I tiptoe down the hall toward the living room.

Court is in a full business suit, pacing around the sofa and coffee table. This room is masculine, with brown leather sofas and dark wood. The only color had been the shiny Bridgerton shelf, which had stuck out, but now is gone. He's goat proofing his place.

I like him a little more than I did before.

He waves at me as he continues his conversation, something about sponsoring a festival in Colorado. That sounds fun. And we could visit. Would he go? I'll have to ask.

I open one side of the French doors to the balcony, and Matilda trots up to me. I take a step out, then hop as I step on something small and hard. Goat pellets, the food kind. They're spilling out of a cloth bag in the far corner.

Rookie mistake, leaving the bag in Matilda's space. She can chew through most containers. "How much did you eat?"

Judging by the poop, more than she should have.

I try to pick up the bag to move it inside, but it's way too heavy. Instant pains shoot up my belly.

There's a broom in the corner that wasn't there before, and the teeth marks on the handle tell me Matilda took an interest in that, too. Court is being so kind to take care of her, but he needs a serious primer on goat habits.

I use the broom to sweep up the poop, then realize he's bought some sort of diaper system. I puzzle out what to do with it when he opens the door. "Just dump it in there and turn the top." Then back on the phone. "Why don't you send the proposal to my assistant Devin?"

I tilt the dustpan into the top of the strangely shaped bucket lined with plastic. Oh, the evil plastic. But I'll do it this once since he asked. I turn the top in the direction of the arrows, and the plastic seals right up, leaving an open space for the next deposit.

Huh. Maybe if we could get compost-degradable bags, it wouldn't be so bad.

There's a water spigot out here, so I rinse off the stiff broom bristles and the dustpan. The water quickly slides off the balcony beneath the wrought-iron railing. Uh oh. I shut it off and peer over the edge. The water falls all the way to the sidewalk below where people are walking.

"Hey!" someone shouts and peers up.

I quickly step back.

"I don't think I'm supposed to run water up here like that," I tell Matilda.

She plops down on the wet concrete.

It's pleasant on the balcony with the fans and the mist. I think of sitting out with her, mainly to keep her out of the bag of pellets, but my stomach growls again.

I'm stuck. I'll have to bother Court.

"Don't eat any more pellets, Matty," I tell her, shaking my finger.

She pays me no mind, lolling on the wet floor.

I step back inside the apartment. I've only taken a couple of squishy steps when I realize my damp feet are leaving dark footprints on the glossy floor. Shoot.

"Don't worry about it," Court says, pocketing the phone. "My housekeeper will be here this afternoon. Are you hungry?"

"I am, but first, can we bring in the bag of pellets? I'm so grateful you found some, but Matilda's eaten through the side of the bag, and she'll gorge herself sick."

"Really?" Court hurries to the door. "Oh." He pulls in the bag, leaving a trail of pellets both outdoors and inside near my footprints. "I should have checked."

"She's fine. I'll milk her shortly."

"I have some pitchers. Take whatever you need." He stands near a round wood dining table at the end of the kitchen. "I had some food delivered. For you, too, not just the goat."

"Her name's Matilda." I slide past him to the refrigerator. It's enormous and bright and filled with every fruit and vegetable I could imagine.

"I got eggs. You eat those, right? The wandering chicken kind. I figured you wouldn't eat the others."

"You mean free-range?" I bite back my smile.

"Yes, that. And three kinds of tofu. I didn't know if you liked it silky or firm. I didn't even know what it meant."

"It's all fine. I'm not picky." I pull an apple out of the fridge and wind up shoving it in my mouth before I can even wash it. I'm too hungry.

"There's a sticker on it," he says, stepping forward to peel it off. "They're organic."

I nod and take another bite on the way to the sink. Only with something in my belly do I manage to pause to wash it. Then I stand there and gobble it down to the stem.

"You were hungry," he says. "Can I make you something?"

"I'm okay." I hold on to the stem.

"Trash is under the sink. You probably compost, don't you?"

"I'll give it to Matilda for a treat. Did we get away clean, or did you hear from the building management?"

He clasps his hands behind his back. "We got away clean. We make good criminals."

I picture him running down the hall, Matilda on his heels. "Maybe in a comedy." I set the apple core on the counter. "So, am I moving somewhere else?"

"Not yet. Devin is working on it. It will probably be Monday."

"Oh. Am I staying here, then?"

"Until some farm thing is over. They filled up a lot of the spots you would have liked. The goat is limiting." He lifts his hands. "Not that she's a problem."

I smile inwardly. He's acting differently this morning. A lot less salty. Almost… concerned.

"There's a farm expo this weekend. Caroline mentioned it."

"Right. That must be the holdup. Will you be okay if I head to the office? I didn't want to leave until you were up and about."

"I'm okay. We'll be fine."

"Good, good. Like I said, Maggie will be here later, so don't be alarmed when she comes in. And I'm a phone call away."

"Did you get your car back?"

"It'll come today. They're driving it here and taking back their car. Devin arranged it."

"Okay, good." The apple has made me even more

hungry, but I don't want to devour half his refrigerator contents in front of him.

He takes a few steps back. This entire exchange has been awkward and different.

"Are you okay, Court?"

"I'm good," he says. "I'll check in with you later." Then he practically bolts out of the kitchen.

I sit at the table and listen as his front door opens, then clicks shut. His apartment is eerily silent and immaculate. The kitchen is cappuccino colored, dark cabinets, light countertops, marbled tile. You could do a cooking show in it with the double ovens, wide steel sinks, and industrial-sized fridge.

A central island has the stove, a griddle, and a cutting board. Pristine pans hang above it in an artful display.

But even so, it doesn't compare to Grandma BeeBee's kitchen, always smelling of garlic and earthy potatoes and something baking all the time. Her cabinets were cluttered with cloth-covered bowls and jars ready for canning or pickling. There was always fruit in baskets and fresh cookies on a plate.

This kitchen is pretty and expensive and clean, a lot like my parents' had been. But it isn't full of life. It isn't home.

I could fix this, but I won't be here longer than a few days.

Even so, maybe I could soften the edges. A bowl of oranges in the corner. A few potatoes in a basket. Maybe a jar with cookies. I wonder if he has ingredients.

A quick look through the cabinets and inside an

expansive pantry tells me that Court has never cooked a day in his life. There's no flour, no oils, no spices of any kind.

He has the utensils, including oven mitts with the tags on them, and all the accessories.

But everything is pre-made, packaged, or ready to eat. I'm guessing he has takeout often.

But I do have milk, butter, and eggs and every vegetable under the sun. He's bought bread and peanut butter.

Peanut butter cookies! I can make those with nothing but egg and a sweetener. I dig into the fridge. Yes, there are dates! I can make date-sweetened peanut butter cookies!

I preheat the oven and hum to myself as I set to chopping and mixing, pausing to cut an avocado in half and scoop the inside directly into my mouth with a spoon.

Soon, the cookies are scooped onto the inaugural use of the nonstick pan and possibly the first pre-heating of the oven.

I mash the second half of the avocado with sprouts and scoop it into celery. I'm eating better than I have since I gave up my yoga job.

My phone buzzes. It's Summer, asking how I'm doing.

*Me: I had to leave the farm. They were using goats for meat!*

*Summer: Oh no!*

*Me: Court came and got me. I'm at his place until they find another farm.*

*Summer: You can't stay there?*

*Me: It's a high rise and no goats allowed!*

*Summer: But this could be it! You two could fall in love and live happily ever after!*

*Me: Not without Matilda.*

Speaking of which, Matilda starts bleating outside, and I'm not sure what to do. I open the door, and she trots inside, heading straight for the bookshelf where the books were.

Court has changed several things, not just moving his books. The jacketed albums are gone as well. Does that mean it's okay for Matilda to be inside?

I hurry her down the hall to my room to get her diaper put on. "It'll be like having a baby here!" I tie the liner and cloth to her. "Let's go back!"

I pat her rump to send her back down the hall to the kitchen. She trots ahead of me, enjoying the space to move, then takes off in a full run.

And that's when I hear a scream.

## 18

## COURT

The frantic call from Maggie comes at the worst moment.

I'm in a meeting with human resources about the results of the external audit of company morale. All those terrible quotes from employees are spread over the table.

Uncle Sherman, the owner of Pickle Media, is in the room. So is his son Jason, my cousin, who keeps throwing me concerned looks as the auditor explains how dire things are at Pickle Media. He seems to think we're months away from a triggering event that could cause a mass exodus.

And my housekeeper won't stop calling.

It has to be about Lucy.

Or her damn goat.

I stand. "I apologize. I have a small matter that's urgent. It will only be a moment."

I take the call as I rush out the door of the boardroom. "What's wrong, Maggie?"

"Sir, sir, Mr. Court. There is a goat in your apartment! It ran straight for me! Holy Mary Mother and Joseph. My life flashed before my eyes."

It's just as I figured. "I'm sorry I didn't warn you."

"You have a goat?"

"I have a guest. And she has a goat."

"I didn't see another person!"

Did Lucy leave with her goat loose in my apartment? "Where are you?"

"In the hall! I can't go in there!"

"Hold on a second."

I put the call on hold and dial Lucy.

It rings. No answer.

There's no telling what has happened. She could be gone. She could have let the phone lose its charge. She could be with her goat, and the phone is in another room.

I return to Maggie. "You know, skip the cleaning. I'll pay you the same. I'll make sure the goat is put away before you come back."

"But I have your groceries!"

"Keep them. Eat them yourself. I had a big delivery last night."

"But your sheets! Your laundry!"

"I'll be all right, Maggie. I promise."

"Okay, Mr. Court. I have time on Sunday."

"Don't waste your weekend on me."

"I don't mind."

"I'm fine. Really." I *have* to return to that meeting.

I shove my phone in my pocket. Back to hell.

I re-enter the room, and the conversation drones on.

Uncle Sherman nods grimly as we're told to hire a specialized company to help boost morale. When we finally adjourn, Uncle Sherman asks to see me privately.

I saw this coming. He and Jason file into my office. When they're inside, I leave my phone with Devin, which I probably should have done before the meeting. "Handle anything that comes down. Lucy and the goat are loose in my apartment."

Devin fails to hide his smirk. He's loving this. "How's Ms. Lucy?"

My tone leaves no room for argument. "Find her a new place."

His smile fades. "Sure, boss."

When I make it into my office, Uncle Sherman and Jason are sitting on the sofa. "Let's order lunch," Uncle Sherman says. "We have things to talk about."

I lower onto an adjacent chair and cross one ankle over my knee. Uncle Sherman is well into his sixties, but he looks like he could block the entire front line of any pro football team. He wears a suit, but no tie, and can look casual no matter what he has on.

Jason is sprawled on his side of his sofa, arms spread across the back. He doesn't bother with suits. He likes his trendy jeans and designer T-shirts that might be more expensive than the furniture he's sitting on. He's expanded his deli in Texas, and now that he's involved in his business, it might be doing better than the flagship one in Manhattan.

"How's Nova?" I ask him.

"Great," he says, but then turns to Sherman.

Something about the timing of me asking about

Nova and him looking to his father sets off an alarm bell. What's this *really* about?

I decide to take control of the conversation before it goes a direction I don't like. "I'll get the takeout menus," I say, but Sherman waves a hand. "Let's cover some ground first."

Oh boy. "Did you want to strategize about the firm coming in without the other members of HR around?"

"No." Sherman leans forward, bracing his elbows on his knees as he clasps his hands together. "This is about a woman and her goat."

Shit. How does he know about this?

I play it cool. "I had a visitor last week. It was a bit of a disruption. But it's handled."

"Handled, how?" Uncle Sherman's voice is steady but firm.

I'm not sure how much I want to reveal. Better to find out what he already knows. "I helped her get settled."

"I hear she's pregnant. Very pregnant."

So he knows a lot. "She is."

"And she says it's yours?"

And there it is. Lucy's pronouncement last week has gotten out. "She is saying so, yes."

"So, how is this handled?" His gaze bores into mine.

"She's at my apartment. We went together to the doctor yesterday. We'll run a paternity test when the baby is born."

"So it could be yours."

"It's a possibility. I met her briefly when I was in Colorado for the New Year."

"Briefly, eh?" Jason says with a laugh.

"Don't be coarse," Sherman booms.

I'm definitely not laughing. "We rang in the New Year together."

"Eight months ago." Sherman taps his shiny black shoes. "How far along is she?"

There's no tiptoeing around this. "Eight months."

He sighs. "What do you know about her?"

"She's a naturalist. Estranged from her family."

"Hmmmph." Sherman sniffs and leans back on the sofa. "Do you get a sense she's after something?"

"I don't think so. She lives very simply in Colorado. I think she just needs somebody."

Jason rubs his chin. "Why wait eight months to turn up?"

"She hadn't planned to tell me."

"Really?" Sherman sits up again. "Why the change?"

"She was going to raise the baby with two friends, but they bailed on her."

"Why was she going to blow you off?" Jason asks.

This I don't know. "Other than the plan with the friends, she hasn't said."

Sherman pours a glass of water from the pitcher on the coffee table. "Well, I'm sure it occurs to you that being a father is a big deal. It will affect everything."

"I will be able to do my job as usual. I assure you of that."

Sherman waves his hand. "I'm not worried about work. But you'll see things differently. And people will see you differently."

"You think being a family man will save morale? Devin suggested that."

He sips the water and shrugs. "Maybe. Maybe not. That's a separate issue. But there will be changes. You do the right thing. No matter what the outcome, you be a credit to the Pickle name."

Jason bites back a smile at that. I stifle any retorts about *his* sullying of the name before he got his act together.

Most of us cousins have had a time of it.

But as Uncle Sherman sorts through takeout menus, I wonder, what does being a credit to the Pickle name really mean for me?

Lucy never picks up a call but later, she texts me that she's fine and sorry she scared the housekeeper.

I unlock the door, opening it carefully in case the goat is close and might try to escape. I've learned my lesson on that.

I hear nothing.

But I smell many things.

Something sweet baking. Something else, too, richer, more savory.

Did Maggie come back? She doesn't normally cook for me.

I walk through the living room. The goat is asleep under the fine mist on the balcony. One of my metal bowls is out there, serving as a food dish. The Dutch oven is in use for water.

I pass the dining room table and turn into the kitchen. Lucy's there, her hair tied up, pulling a tray of cookies out of the oven.

"You're home!" She sets the tray on the side of the stove not taken up by pots. Two things are cooking.

"You're being domestic."

"I so rarely get to cook in a proper kitchen. I only have a propane stove in my yurt. This is a real treat."

She stares down at her oven mitts as she places them on the counter. "I really am sorry I scared your house-keeper away."

"The goat charged her?"

"I didn't realize she had come in. I'm so sorry, Court. I should have kept Matilda on the balcony."

"It's all right. We'll arrange it better next time."

Her gaze meets mine at the "next time." And she's right. She won't be here long enough for a next time.

Although she might be back if the baby turns out to be mine.

I press the heel of my hand to my forehead, Uncle Sherman's words weighing on me. *Be a credit to the Pickle name.*

"Did Devin find a new farm for us?" Lucy asks.

I drop my arm. If Lucy wants to go to a farm, then surely sending her is the right thing. It has to be hard on her goat to sit on a balcony.

"We were pretty overwhelmed with an issue at work, but he's hoping to comb through what's available after this farming event that has everything booked."

"Oh." She picks up a spatula and moves the cookies to a plate. "What's happening at work?"

I loosen my tie. "Just some employee reviews. I'm going to change."

"Okay! I made peanut butter cookies, and I've got some potatoes on to boil for a casserole with leeks and mushrooms."

I bought leeks? I don't even know what they are. "That sounds good."

"What do you normally eat?" she asks.

I shrug, sliding off my suit jacket. "Whatever takeout sounds good."

She nods. "I thought so. This will be better."

Will it? I guess I'll find out. If it's a total bust, I'll make an excuse and grab a slice at Luciano's Pizzeria up the street.

I take one more glance at her as I head down the hall. She's wearing the yellow dress and the shoes I got her all cleaned up from yesterday's mishap. Her neck is long and exposed with her hair up. The warmth of the kitchen gives her a rosy glow.

No woman has ever set foot in there, at least other than Maggie.

It's nice.

And I don't like thinking about it being nice.

## 19

## LUCY

I'm not the most amazing cook in the world, but I have a lot of fresh ingredients and the internet to search for recipes.

I stare at my phone, making sure I prepare the casserole precisely as the video shows.

I want this to be exactly right. I'm so upset that I scared off Court's housekeeper. I tried to call after her, but I didn't dare open the front door after she fled, as Matilda was determined to get out.

"Learning something new?"

Court's voice is so close and so startling that I jump back from the stove, straight into his chest.

His arms go around me as he laughs. "Sorry. I'm stealthy. You okay?" He makes sure I have my footing before letting me go. He has socks and a pair of sneakers in one hand.

"Yes. I didn't hear you at all." I glance down at his bare feet. For the first time, I'm the one in shoes. I like it. He has strong man feet, sturdy legs, and bulging thigh muscles disappear into what appear to be workout shorts.

I'm staring.

I whip around to face the stove. "I need to put it in." Oh, God. That sounds so wrong. "The casserole. Into the oven. It's going in the oven." I'm a stammering mess.

He doesn't seem to notice. "Do I have time to hit the gym downstairs?"

"About an hour."

"That's perfect then." He sits at the table, pulling on his socks.

I watch him from the corner of my eye, sprinkling shredded cheese on top of the casserole for the final step.

He stands. "I'll be back."

"Hey, can I get a clarification on something?"

He pauses by the end of the counter. He's something, his hair askew, a fitted T-shirt stretching over his chest, the shorts. Those strong legs. I feel a little wobbly.

"Sure."

"Matilda. Is she confined to the balcony?"

He shrugs. How can a shrug be so sexy? "You obviously let her in here earlier."

"It's just—you put away the books and albums, and it seemed like a few other things as though you expected her inside."

"I did some basic goat proofing." He glances around. "There's probably more she could get into unsupervised."

"Oh, I would never give her the run of the place. But if she's sitting with me?"

"Sure. It's not goat jail."

I open my mouth to thank him, but he's already gone. The front door opens, then closes.

It feels lonelier than it did before. I examine the spread of cheese on the dish, convinced that if only I make this perfect, everything will somehow work out between us. I'm not looking to be his wife or great love. But forging a light, easy relationship before the baby comes will help smooth things over when the paternity test shows the baby is his.

And it will.

I slide the casserole into the oven and open the door to the balcony. "Come on, little one. We can hang out until Court gets back."

Matilda lifts her head, eyes half-closed, then drops it down again. She likes her misty spot. Probably the outdoors feels better to her, even on concrete. We need hay. I wish I could walk her so she could eat shrubbery and forage, but in the city, she might eat someone's garden or decor.

Manhattan is no place for a goat. And getting her downstairs could tip off the neighbors, who might report it.

No, we're stuck.

I close the door and wander the living room for the hundredth time. Court moved several items, evidenced by the blank spots on his bookshelf. But he left anything high and out of Matilda's reach. There are more books, a mixture of fiction and... huh. A ton of carpentry manuals.

I read through the titles. Tables. Chairs. Decorative boxes. He has three on bed frames. I pull one out and open it. Sawdust drifts from the pages.

He used these. Or someone did.

Many of the books show the wear and tear of being propped open, particularly on pages demonstrating tricky techniques for complex detailing. I laugh when it appears an entire pot of wood stain was spilled on one section, gluing the pages together.

I set them back and wander the room. What I look for, and don't find, are photos. None of his family. No friends. No picnics or coworkers or out with buddies. Other than the well-loved carpentry books, this could be a staged home for a decorator or real estate agent.

I've wandered through his living room, dining area, kitchen, and my bedroom and bath. There's an extra bathroom in the hall with a nautical theme and two closed doors. I assume one is a closet, but based on the placement of the other, it has to be another bedroom. I wonder what he uses it for and briefly picture the red room from *Fifty Shades of Grey*.

The door to his bedroom is open, but I don't linger there. It feels like snooping. A glance inside tells me he doesn't make his bed, which is at least one glitch in his perfect home. But it's as impersonal as every other room, all black and silver.

His gleaming bureau is uncluttered.

I hurry back to the kitchen, not wanting to be caught looking, even for a second. I put together a salad from the vegetables, taking my time with washing and chopping each item.

Who is this man, really?

The front door opens. I step to the end of the kitchen to look through the living room. I catch only a glimpse of his sweaty form before he's down the hall. My heart hammers painfully, and I press my hand to my chest. We're alone in his place, and unlike last night, I'm awake. And cooking.

What will happen?

My mind spins with wild scenarios, sex on the counters, falling onto the sofa. I return to that night on New Year's Eve. He'd been passionate but controlled.

I'd still liked it.

But that's far removed from our situation. I shouldn't even think of it.

The timer dings, and I check on the casserole. It's brown and bubbly, and my head swims just looking at it. Unending hunger. That's been my pregnancy.

I reach up for the dinner plates, but between my belly and the height, even tiptoe isn't quite enough. I stretch my fingers as high as I can.

"I'll get those."

Court's low rumble sends vibrations through me. I can smell him so distinctly, all fresh herbal shampoo and masculine soap. My body hums with his nearness as he reaches up beside me to bring down the plates.

"Smells good," he says. "I've never had leeks. I'm not even sure what they are."

This makes me laugh. "You bought them!"

"I was grabbing everything that looked Lucy-like."

"Leeks are Lucy-like?"

"They must have been."

I turn to the fridge and pull out the extras. "These are leeks."

"Oh! I thought those were green onions on steroids."

I laugh again. "It's the same family of plants. They're easy to grow."

"Have you? Grown them?"

"Sure. Colorado has great growing seasons. I raise potatoes, parsley, tomatoes, watermelon, radishes, beets."

"You eat beets?"

"You don't?"

He sniffs at the casserole. "I might eat *your* beets."

I absolutely shiver at the words. If he'd been some other man, and I wasn't in such a vulnerable, precarious situation, I would have let the sexual banter begin.

But I simply say, "That's a great compliment for someone who hasn't even tried my cooking yet."

"I have faith." He opens several drawers before finding a serving spoon. He's clearly unfamiliar with his own kitchen. He does at least know the location of the silverware, proving he doesn't rely on disposable plastic forks.

He fills two glasses with filtered water while I serve up the casserole and salad.

"I bought bread. It's somewhere." He opens the pantry and sorts through the shelves.

"It's in the bread box."

He leans out of the pantry. "I have a breadbox?"

I laugh again. "It's the pretty wood box about shoulder high on the right."

He brings the whole thing out. "Huh. I wondered what this was for. The decorator bought it." He lifts the front panel. "It looked like a tiny roll-top desk for a cat or something."

Now I'm giggling hard enough to get on a roll. I hold my belly, picturing a cat jotting his memoirs beside the bread box.

Court shakes his head at me and takes our plates to the table. "You laugh a lot."

I squeak out, "You laugh too little."

"Probably so."

We sit down opposite each other, and everything feels so comfortable, so right, that I am momentarily disoriented, like I've stepped into some other life.

I wait anxiously as Court stabs a forkful of the casserole. "I didn't ask if you were allergic to anything, or disliked it," I say. "There are mushrooms."

"I'm good with anything. And I didn't ask you either."

"You knew I was vegetarian."

He grins, and his face is so transformed that I feel like I've gone underwater.

He takes a bite and closes his eyes.

I slowly slide my fork through the potatoes, waiting for his verdict.

Finally, he groans and says, "This is heavenly."

I let out a long rush of air. Thank goodness. My appetite comes roaring forward, and I shovel a hefty forkful into my mouth. "Ooooh, yes," I say, then blush because I'm afraid that the way it sounded is all too similar to my tone with him on New Year's Eve. In bed. During orgasm.

He doesn't notice. "I'm going to eat all of this and more."

I wiggle in my seat with happiness. This is going well. It's about time we had something good between us.

But then he asks a question that seems so simple but is anything but.

"So, how did you end up becoming a vegetarian?"

And suddenly, I'm not hungry.

## 20

## COURT

The moment I ask the question, I know it's the wrong one.

Lucy's happy expression dissolves. She pokes at her food with her fork.

I decide to pivot. "Never mind. It's fine. How's Matilda holding up?"

Lucy bites her lip, but she answers. "She's good. She likes the mist."

I regret trying to make small talk. This is why I don't have women over. Or anyone over. I'm shit at this.

The room rings with the sounds of our silverware stabbing the plates in the silence.

I scoot my chair back, planning to make an excuse to hole up in my bedroom.

But Lucy speaks, so low that I almost don't hear her. "It was my Grandma BeeBee."

I lean forward. "BeeBee?"

"Her real name was Beatrice, but I couldn't pronounce that when I was little."

"Cute."

"She was my father's mother. She had a small farm. It had been bigger, back when my grandfather was alive, but she'd sold off pieces of it every few years so she could pay the taxes on the part she lived on."

Lucy's face relaxes as she talks about this woman.

"She grew most everything she ate. She had goats." Lucy's smile grows wide as she remembers the good parts. "And a cow, also named Beatrice. Always. Lots of different cows I remember, and they were always Beatrice."

"Her little joke?"

"She was very self-deprecating." Lucy takes a long drink of water, and I'm mesmerized by the movements of her long, tender throat.

"You two were close?"

She nods. "I practically lived over there. We grew plants. Pickled and preserved everything from jam to radishes."

"Was your dad not like her?"

Lucy shakes her head. "Not in the least. It's like he tried to be the opposite. I was the only one in the family who felt the same as she did about the earth."

"She sounds special." I don't want to ask if she's around. It's clear she's not.

Lucy confirms it. "She was. She died while I was in college. My father had Beatrice the Eighth cut into steaks and put BeeBee's farm on the market to be sold to a strip mall developer."

I sit up. "He didn't ask if you wanted it?"

"He's a commercial real estate agent. BeeBee's farm was probably a real feather in his cap."

Now her eyes glisten.

"Oh, Lucy. I'm sorry. Did it get built?"

She shrugs. "I don't know. I refuse to drive out there and look. It's outside Louisville. I can't bear to see it. I want to remember it as it was."

"I passed through that area last year. There's farmland out there."

"But the city was encroaching." She returns to dragging her fork through the casserole.

I run the back of my hand over my beard. So, this is her fallout with her parents. "What about your mom?"

"She's a petroleum engineer!" Lucy's lips press tightly together. "It's like he married someone as far from BeeBee as he could get!"

"Were you vegetarian when you were a kid?"

"As soon as I could protest. Age six or so. They went to great lengths to fool me. Grinding up meat and mixing it in my soups. Lying about the ingredients in pretty much everything. It's like they thought I was judging them for eating meat. I don't care who eats meat. I just don't want to. The farm was the last resort."

"Did you ask your dad about buying it yourself?"

"I begged him to hold onto it until I got a job. I would pay for it. I would find a way. But he didn't want me living out there. He wanted me to have a big-city job, like my brother. I was majoring in finance because that's what he would help me pay for."

Another mystery explained. "What does your brother do?"

Lucy shakes her head, setting her fork down. "He's a crypto, blockchain, tech bro."

"And Dad is proud?"

"Totally. He thinks he's cutting edge."

"When was the last time you talked to them?"

"Graduation. I didn't invite them, but they showed up anyway."

"How long was that after BeeBee…"

"Her funeral? About four months. When I first saw them there, I was stupidly hopeful, like maybe he'd give me the deed to her farm as a graduation gift."

"And he didn't."

"He offered me a job at his company! Buying and selling more strip malls!" She pushes a hunk of hair behind her ear. "I took off. I didn't answer their calls. And I never took a job in finance."

"Have you been living in a yurt all this time?"

"No. I lived with April and Summer until I got Matilda. In school, I had an internship as a clerk in a small accounting office, and I stayed there awhile after graduation. But then I got tired of being around people who worried so much about money. So I left and added more yoga classes to my roster."

"And then you came to the Castle Hotel for New Year's Eve."

"And then I met you. Yes."

I sip my water. "Hard to say which of these events was the most impactful."

"Oh, you, by a long shot. There has never been three minutes of my time that was more life changing."

"Three minutes!" I sit up. "What are you talking about? We were in that room for hours!"

She laughs at that, and despite the insult, I'm relieved to see her recovering from talking about hard things.

"You are too easy to tweak, Court Armstrong. But the most critical part was maybe thirty seconds."

"You think the condom was defective?"

"Did anything seem wrong with it when you took it off?"

I think back. I remember pulling out of her and grabbing a Kleenex from a box on the side table. "I didn't inspect it. Did you feel extra juicy?"

She bites her lip again. "I was, uh, pretty wet already."

My dick stirs at that. "I seem to recall that."

"It was pretty hot, the whole thing."

"It was."

She fiddles with the linen napkin in her lap. "I don't usually do things like that."

"And here we are."

"Here we are." She meets my gaze, and I wonder if she's thinking about that night. I sure as hell am.

She's not far. I could reach out and touch her easily. Run my fingers up her arm. Tangle them in her hair. Bring her face to mine.

I'm already cock-deep in the memory of her at the doctor's office, naked, glowing, round and soft. My hands twitch with the need to travel over the mound of her belly.

She's here. We could test this thing. See what else there might be.

We stare at each other. Is she leaning in? What can we even do? Would sex hurt the baby? Does she want that?

Would it complicate things?

I'm on the verge of reaching for her, when she blurts, "I appreciate you letting me stay nearby until the baby is born. I understand you need proof."

Right, proof.

I wait a second, see if we can slide back into the magic, but she's looking away, her foot tapping anxiously on the floor.

The moment has passed. I probably imagined it. "It's fine. We'll get you situated on a farm again once that big expo or whatever is over."

"Caroline invited me to that."

"Did you want to go?"

"I did, but I couldn't go with her knowing about the operation at the back of her farm."

That makes sense. "What do you want, Lucy? How do you see this playing out?"

Her brows draw together. "I don't know."

"You must have had some idea as you were traveling several days to get here."

Her laugh is rueful. "I think I was just trying to get from moment to moment during that. But I wondered what it would be like to meet you again. I remembered you as being gruff."

I kick back in my chair. "I've been told that."

"What makes Court so salty?"

*Not going there.*

I stand and pick up my plate. "You want more? Are you done?"

She scoots the plate closer to me.

I take both of them to the sink to rinse them.

She keeps sitting at the table. I don't normally do anything with my dishes. I have so few of them that I leave them for Maggie to handle. I'm not even sure how to turn the dishwasher on.

There's salad in the bowl and casserole in the dish. I should cover them with something and store it. Plastic wrap? No, Lucy will protest. I should have aluminum foil. Maybe.

Lucy walks over. "I'll handle this."

"There are no gender roles here."

"No, but there's competence and incompetence."

I'm about to make a gruff retort, but I stop myself. She's right. "I don't eat here very often. But my mother made us wash dishes. I know how to do that."

"Good." She turns on the water and closes the drain. "Find a clean dish towel, and you can dry."

I open drawers, relieved we've found our way beyond another impasse.

Life sure looks different from what it was a week ago.

I guess I can make some sort of effort.

## 21

### LUCY

I struggle to fall asleep that night, thinking over the moment when I triggered Court to abruptly end our conversation at dinner.

I should have known that asking what makes him salty isn't equivalent to him asking what made me vegetarian. But I suspect the answers are equally deep.

My family hurt me. They never saw me for who I was. My dad, in rejecting his mother, rejected me. Even marrying my mom was thumbing his nose at everything his parents had stood for. And that doesn't even touch what he did to BeeBee's farm.

It's why I chose Court over them. Besides, Dad knows lots of lawyers in his business, and my greatest fear of all is that if they decide their grandbaby would be better off with them, they might find a way to take him.

Or her.

Lately, I've had dreams about a little girl. She likes to wear overalls and run barefoot in the grass. But when I place a crown of flowers on her head, the sun striking her light hair makes her look like a princess.

I wake up with a start. Something's banging against the door.

There's a snorting sound.

That's not Court.

"Matilda?"

*Eh heh heh.*

It is Matilda!

I throw open the door.

Matilda is there, not wearing a diaper.

"That's risky inside," I say and lead her into my room. I snatch up the liner and diaper set that dried overnight in my bathroom and strap it on.

Then I sit cross-legged on the floor in front of her in my goat T-shirt and yoga shorts rolled below my belly. "What are you doing inside?" I ask her.

Court pauses in the open door, looking outrageously gorgeous in nothing but loose gray shorts and a plain white T-shirt. His hair is tousled, and his beard isn't smoothed. "She looked too forlorn out there."

I force myself not to stare at him. "Did she poop everywhere?"

"Only twice. Luckily, it's all tile inside."

It's true. It's easy to clean. "I'll get it."

"Already done." He passes me a small plate of toast spread with butter. "I was going to do goat cheese, but then I read pregnant women can't eat unpasteurized cheese."

I take the plate. "You were reading up?"

He shrugs. "Casual curiosity."

"Was it?" I take a bite of toast, lifting it high to keep Matilda out of it. I don't realize how hungry I am until I've gobbled the entire piece.

"Do you eat your own goat cheese?" he asks. "Like you know it's safe, so you eat it?"

"I did before I came to New York. Matilda wasn't around other livestock, and it was reasonable that she didn't have listeriosis, which is what they're worried about. But since we traveled, and then she got penned with other goats, I've stopped."

"Do they make safe goat cheese? Do you miss it?"

"It's fine. I can wait another month."

He takes the empty plate from me. "I'll make more. There's some cheddar in there. Hard cheese is okay, the docs say. You want that?"

I nod. "And some fruit?"

"You got it. Do you drink coffee, or is that bad? I didn't see it listed specifically."

"That's a moderation thing, but I don't drink it. I'm more about tea."

"Tea. Do I have any tea?"

I laugh. "Yes, you have chamomile and Earl Grey in your pantry, on the right."

"You already know this place better than I do." He takes off down the hall.

I hold Matilda's cheeks and kiss her nose. "What's up with him? Is it opposite day? Salty becomes sweet?"

Matilda licks my chin in response. Only when I rub her ears do I realize there's something tied around her neck.

It's a ribbon. I pull on it, and it comes undone, the bow unlacing in my hands.

The ribbon slides through the partially sealed flap of an envelope. I pull it apart, and the ribbon falls free.

Matilda noses it, ready to chomp. I tug it away. "Let's not eat that."

I pull out two plastic passes. I flip one over.

### *FARM EXPO VIP*
#### *ENTRANCE TO ALL EXHIBITS AND PRIVATE SHOWINGS*

What?

I try to jump to my feet, but my belly has other ideas. I wrestle myself to standing by using the bedpost.

I hurry to the kitchen, where Court is examining an electric teakettle.

"The expo?" I hold out the passes.

He glances over, then returns to the kettle. "I didn't want you to miss it because of Caroline. Thought you could pick up some milking supplies. Maybe find some customers."

My eyes smart, hard and sharp. I throw my arms around him. "Court!"

He pats my shoulder. "I rented another SUV with a big dog package in the back so Matilda could go along safely."

I pull back. Big, fat tears drip down my face. "Really?"

"I don't know what a goat cheese operation needs, but it seems like it's more than what you have in your knapsack."

I nod. "You don't have to."

"You're here a month. Might as well make the most of Matilda's assets." He finds the power button. "Ah, there." The kettle kicks on, and the water temperature on the digital display instantly climbs.

"Okay!" I haven't been to any farming event since…

Since Grandma BeeBee was alive.

"Oh, and I called that Natural Outfitter place." He says this casually, as if he's not about to drop a big ol' bombshell. "They said they would open an hour early for us so you could pick out some more clothes. I promised a *Pretty Woman* level spend for their trouble."

"Court!"

"I'll finish breakfast. Get yourself ready to go."

I hurry back to my room. I'm going to the Expo! And shopping!

Matilda watches me as I rush to turn on the shower. I kiss her head. "We get to go to the Expo! In new clothes!"

And admittedly, as the water runs down my face, I end up shedding a lot more tears, for BeeBee, for me, and for this strange, salty man who can sometimes be the kindest person I know.

## 22

## COURT

Who knew cargo capris could be kinda hot?

Lucy twirls in a peachy-melon pair with a clingy white top that the sales lady has assured her will stretch and then revert to its previous shape with washing.

After seeing her in nothing but flowy dresses and an oversized T-shirt, watching her roll down the waistband of the cargos and tuck in the tight shirt is unexpectedly sexy. The heathery-textured top emphasizes the womanly shape of her breasts and belly.

When she asks me, "What do you think?" I'm unexpectedly tongue tied.

She frowns and crosses her hands over her stomach. "It's too much, isn't it? I should stick to dresses."

I clear my throat. "No, no. It's a great look. You're showing off that baby."

She turns back to the mirror. "It's so comfortable. I've been awfully tired of dresses."

"Get every color," I tell her.

The sales assistant holds up a pink and green camouflage pattern.

"Except that one," I add.

Lucy giggles. "I don't think that camo will hide anyone anywhere."

"It's meant to be seen," the woman says but switches it out for a traditional khaki pair.

"That's better," Lucy says. "But only two. The ones I'm wearing and those."

"We have a minimum spend, you know," I tell her, although really, we don't.

She turns in front of the mirror. "You're terribly generous."

It's been a good morning. I woke up feeling different. Like, tired of her suffering. Crap family. Hard life. Knocked up.

I want to fix everything.

She seems so happy.

Her happiness feels good.

"Try on some more," I tell her. "I want to see you in those short shorts. I seem to remember those thighs."

She leans over to smack my shoulder. "Court!"

The sales woman smiles. "I predict a lot more babies where that one came from!" Then she hustles off to pull the shorts.

Lucy sits beside me on the bench. "That's an interesting thing for her to say. Do you think we're acting like a couple?"

"I think I'm acting like a sugar daddy."

She smacks me again. "Like I would ever have one of those!" She fingers the various pockets down her legs.

"I had to give up most of my clothes when I moved into the yurt. There isn't a lot of space, and I only had two trunks that sealed tightly enough to keep the bugs out."

This makes me grimace. "Everything you own is in the yurt?"

"It is. I stored some things at April and Summer's place, but then they both left."

"Does your yurt lock? Is someone stealing everything you own right now?"

She shrugs. "It's made of canvas. There's no point in locking it even if I could. You can slit the side. I don't have anything valuable. No electronics or jewelry."

"Is the yurt hidden?"

"Totally. It's in the foothills on private property." She laughs. "I have more to worry from raccoons and termites."

I have so many questions about how she stores food and where she showers, but the woman returns with several colors of shorts. "These the ones?"

"Looks good," I say and help Lucy up with a boost to her waist. "Let me know if you get tired. We can always rest before we go."

"I can sleep in the car!" she says.

"Where you two headed?" the woman asks.

"The Farm Expo." Lucy takes one pair of shorts and heads into the changing room.

The woman tilts her head. "Where's that?"

"Upstate," I say. "They show animals and have vendors and booths."

"Sounds fun." She hangs the extra colors of the shorts on the rack. "What else should I look for?"

"Comfortable things. I think the pregnancy is going to get harder before it's done."

The woman nods. "She didn't want regular maternity clothes?"

"She's so close to the end. She's particular about companies and fabrics."

"She's in the right place."

Lucy comes out in the shorts, showing miles of leg. "I can't button these either, but they tuck nicely. They'll be good transition shorts after the baby comes."

"Turn around," I tell her.

She blushes but makes a circle. The shorts cup her ass just above the start of those thighs I can't stop staring at. Now I'm picturing her in them but topless.

*Cool your jets, Court.*

"They look good," I say.

She tries to peer over her shoulder to see the back of them in the mirror. "I'll have to take your word for it."

We try on sneakers until she finds a pair that makes her cry out with pleasure. "They feel like clouds!" She speed-walks around the store. "My feet will never hurt again!"

I wonder how much she has endured lately. The belly pains. One pair of worn-out shoes.

If I have anything to say about it, she'll have everything.

We make one more pass through the store, grabbing socks, underwear, more T-shirts, and another dress like the one I got her, only pale pink.

"Last night, I dreamed the baby was a girl," she says as we head to the counter.

"Despite the string test?"

"It's just a dream."

"Not nearly as reliable as a string test." I shake my head.

The woman rings us up. "My mama was big into that black magic witchy stuff. She says if your pupils dilate when you look in a mirror, it's a boy."

"Really?" Lucy's gaze flicks toward a sunglass display with a mirror.

I chuckle. "Go on. Try it." I'd prefer she be away from the register at totaling time, anyway. I don't want her to feel like she's not worth the amount, and she will. She always does.

I wonder when was the last time someone spoiled her?

Probably not since she lost her grandmother. That woman lavished her with time and love and teaching. Those are the best expenditures. I knew it once, too.

I shake that off.

While Lucy peers into the sunglass mirror, I quickly pass the woman a credit card.

"How dilated are we talking?" Lucy calls.

"Beats me!" the woman calls back.

Lucy takes out her phone. "I'm googling it."

I tuck my card back in my wallet. "I'd trust black magic over Google these days."

"Same." The woman passes me three large bags. "Have fun with the farmers."

We take our time strolling to the apartment building. Lucy holds my arm so she can walk with her face upturned to the morning light, her eyes closed.

There aren't many people downtown on a Saturday morning, mostly dog walkers from the nearby high rises. But they spot her belly, and all my bags, and smile at us. We must be the picture of expectant couple bliss.

I try putting that role on for a minute. Lucy is my wife. Our firstborn is about to arrive. We've been in love for ages. This is our neighborhood, our life.

To be honest, it doesn't feel too bad.

## 23

## LUCY

Sneaking a goat down the stairs is much easier than going up the elevator. In my new tennis shoes, peachy cargo Capri pants, and the snug white shirt, I feel like a completely new person.

I use the collar and leash rather than the lead with the loop since there might be huge distractions to set Matilda off running. I have no idea what to expect, but I'm super excited.

The drive out to Syracuse is sunny and beautiful. The trees shimmer with vibrant green, and the highway is shiny, like a silver ribbon threading through the scenery.

Court is relaxed behind the wheel, his strong features in profile against the brightness of the window. I have to stop myself from squealing every time I think about what we're doing together and everything he planned for me today.

Nobody since BeeBee has given me a day like this.

"You never said how your dilation gender prediction came out," he says.

"Oh, hush. You're making fun of me."

"No, no. I find these old wives' tales interesting. They have to come from something."

"No dilation."

"Does that mean girl or boy?"

"Girl, if you believe a store employee."

"Uh oh."

"What?" I turn to him.

He's laughing. "That means you have a direct contradiction between your two forms of gender divination. The string says a boy. Dilation says a girl."

"Maybe it's twins." I smirk in satisfaction when his face pales.

"You think?"

"No, no. I had a sonogram. There's only one baby in there."

"And they didn't tell you the gender?"

"He was turned the wrong way. And it's, you know, one of those freebie clinics for people who can't pay. They don't take much time." I try to say it simply, because I don't want him to feel sorry for me. I made my choices.

"Will the sonogram you do next week be like that, short, with a side of humiliation?" His voice is harsh.

"I'm grateful I could get one. Grateful for the program. For my ability to get through the paperwork. To be approved. That's more privilege than some expectant mothers have."

His frown deepens. "But next week?"

I shrug. "It might be pricey. My program was for Colorado, so it doesn't apply here."

"It'll be fine." He waves off my concern. "I mainly want you to feel like you got the information you went in for. The reassurance."

"The baby kicks, so I feel good about it. I'm healthy, and I haven't had any complications other than these ligament pains. And being endlessly hungry and thirsty."

"Are you now? Hungry and thirsty?"

"I can wait until we get there. I looked it up. They have tons of food booths. And a whole tent devoted to preserves and canning. You can buy almost anything in a jar. If they have bearberry jam, you'll have to stand aside while I shove my paw in the jar and eat it straight off my fingers."

"Now that's an image." He says it low and rumbly, like I was talking about sex.

I mean, maybe it's a little sexy, licking jam off your fingers.

Then I picture Court licking jam off his fingers.

Then other things off his fingers.

He'd done that on New Year's Eve.

My body flashes hot.

I press my hand to my chest.

"You okay?" he asks. "Are you in pain? Contractions?"

"No, no. I'm fine." My cheeks heat up. "I'm pretty sturdy."

"Okay. If you're sure."

"I'm sure." He's being very doting this morning.

"So, what do bearberries taste like?"

I'm relieved to get my mind off the dirty thoughts. "They look like blueberries, tiny ones, but they taste more like apples. Bears love them. You can eat them straight off the bush. They unfortunately look a lot like some of the poisonous berries out there. But BeeBee taught me how to find them. If bears can do it, surely humans can."

"Did she have them on her farm?"

"In the woods beyond it." I frown. "Those are probably mowed down too by now."

He signals, and we shift from one highway to another. I turn to take a peek at Matilda. She's standing in the back of the SUV, seeming to enjoy the height she has to easily look out the window. She's more dog-like than I had imagined.

"We should get some hay for her," I say. "If it's okay to spread it on your balcony."

"Sure."

"Probably just a bale if I'm leaving Monday."

"We'll get a couple in case Devin has trouble finding you a place."

"Will it be near the other farm? I picked that doctor because it was close."

"We'll have to figure that out as we go."

Traffic suddenly picks up, which seems unexpected for a Saturday. As we exit again, this time for a smaller road, it's jammed with trucks and trailers.

"I think we've found your people," Court says.

A sign reads, "Farm Expo parking one mile ahead."

"Ooooh." I press my hands to the glass, looking out. There are too many trees to see anything.

But soon, we approach cleared land and miles of gravel. A man in an orange vest waves at us to park in a row.

Court pulls up to him. "Where's VIP parking?"

"Keep going to the front. There's a row of golf carts. You have your cart number?"

Court nods.

"You got a golf cart?" I ask.

"It comes with the top tier passes."

I inspect mine. There are numbers on the back. One line says Cart 53. "How did you get these in time?"

"I had a courier pick them up and deliver them."

"We could have gotten them when we arrived!"

He grins as he turns the wheel down the first row, right next to a big open gate with a huge "Farm Expo" sign. "But then I couldn't have surprised you."

A gesture. He's doing a gesture.

But why?

I shake off the question. *Just accept it, Lucy.*

Another man with a flag waves us to our spot. When we get out, he calls, "You know your cart number?"

"Fifty-three!" I yell back.

He gives us a thumb's up.

We unload Matilda from the back.

"If she hates the cart, we can walk," Court says.

"Oh, she'll love it. Before I got too pregnant, we would do some odd jobs for the woman who owns the property my yurt is on. We got around on her four-wheeler."

"What kind of jobs?"

I tie Matilda's leash through a loop on the floor of the cart. She pokes her head between us on the front seat. "Moving brush. Mending pens. She had chickens. We tended them when she was gone."

"Was that in exchange for rent?"

"Some. I also gave her goat cheese."

"Did you use her bathroom, too?"

"No, I would shower and things at the yoga studio."

He leans on the steering wheel. "So, when you couldn't teach anymore, you were out of running water."

I pet Matilda's head. "And I came here. Like I said, I got to the end of my rope."

"So, you peed in the woods?"

I laugh. "You're obviously not much of a camping person."

His face is contorted as he punches the code from the back of his badge to turn on the cart. "We did that, sure. My parents were outdoorsy. My brother is a serious hiker."

"Okay, then, you know how it works."

"But a weekend is different from all the time."

"It wasn't all that long. Summer only left for Vegas two months ago. I had access to her place until then."

He shakes his head. "You're made of pretty stern stuff."

I hope he means that in a good way, not a weird one. I'm very aware that how I lived was unusual. I just got… stuck.

Court twists around to look behind him as he

prepares to back out of the spot. I wrap an arm around Matilda's neck to keep her steady. She lets out a happy *meh eh eh*.

"Me too, Matilda. Me, too."

The gravel crunches beneath the tires as we approach the entry. We don't even need to flash our passes. I guess the golf cart tells the story. We're waved through a gate and wow! Huge white tents have been erected on the back side, like it's a circus. Shiny green tractors line up like giants.

We drive along the big rig row, admiring a long red rotary tiller tearing up a patch of dirt while several men in ball caps watch.

We turn down a row of temporary pens, the silver bars winking in the sun. There are entire herds here. Cows. Sheep. And goats!

"Look, Matilda! There are more Nubians like you!"

Matilda pays me no mind, snorting at the air.

I glance around to see what she's picking up on.

A big hay baler is sitting ahead, and a man is turning the flywheel to show how the claws drag in loose hay to push through the machine and bundle it into perfect rectangles wrapped with twine.

Matilda smells the hay.

Court leans over. "You think he'll sell us some?"

"I think it's a manufacturer, not a farmer, but maybe!"

Court pulls up next to the baler. Several of the men look at Matilda with amusement as I untie the leash and let her walk on the ground. She immediately scarfs up bits of hay that blow near her hooves.

"We got a cleaner upper," one man calls. "We could use a goat to hoover up our mess!"

"She's doing it!" I holler back.

One of the men steps forward to shake Court's hand. I can't hear their conversation over the *chunk, chunk* sounds of the baler. Matilda makes a happy leap in the air, then returns to eating hay as fast as she can.

Court comes over. "He says we can come by later and grab a couple of bales. They're going to have more than they want to haul home."

"How nice of them!" I wave at the cluster of men.

"Are we going to be able to get her back on the cart with all this food around?" Court asks.

"I'll get her going. Goats aren't really grazers. They like to eat brush at head level if they can. If you hold some hay out, she'll prefer that." I bend down to gather up some hay, but Court stops me.

"Let me do that." He collects a good cluster and holds it out to Matilda. When she starts chewing, he walks backward toward the cart, bringing her with him.

When we're back in the cart, Matilda still happily chewing, I tell him, "See, you're going to be a goat expert before this is over."

"Do you want to look at the other goats?" he asks.

"No, that might agitate Matilda if they are uncut males. Can we head to the tents?"

"Anything the lady wants."

I try to hold back my squeal as we approach the long tent, open on one side. There's an unending line of crafters with everything from quilts to jams to pies to pickles to embroidery to jewelry.

I can't stop myself. "Squeeeee!"

Court laughs. "Get one of everything."

"I won't have space in my yurt!"

He averts his gaze at that, and I realize I probably won't be going back to the yurt. Not once he realizes the baby is his.

Will I live in his fancy apartment? I can't do that to Matilda. The balcony is fine for a while but not long term. Besides, he's sure to get caught with her there.

I refuse to think about it. Today is for fun. Court is giving me everything I want.

We park with a cluster of other golf carts at the end of the tent. I untether Matilda again.

"I'll take her," Court says. "You roam the stalls."

The first woman sits behind her tables piled high with shopping bags woven from recycled plastic. "Carry things with confidence," she says as she holds up one of her bags. "I like to start things off because you can then fill up your bag as you go!"

"That's so smart! How much are they?" I could use at least one.

I reach into my pocket, but Court's there. "We'll get four for starters." He passes her a credit card, then guides Matilda away from the tablecloth she's about to chomp.

The woman waves at her stacks. "Pick any four you like."

I pick one made mostly of pink and white bags with a pink braided handle.

"Are you having a girl?" the woman asks.

"We're finding out in a few days."

"How lovely." She finds a similar bag in tones of blue. "Better cover your bases!"

I'm not much for color coding humans, but the blue bags are pretty, so I choose one. Then a couple of wildly mixed colors. "Thank you. These look sturdy."

"They'll last forever!" She passes me the credit card. "For your husband."

I almost tell her he's not but then decide there's no reason to do so. "Thank you." I string the four bags on one arm as I head to the open side to return the card.

"Keep that," Court says. "We're going to walk outside of the tent to avoid getting into trouble."

I laugh. "Good idea."

It's nice having him watch Matilda as I peruse the booths. I buy practical things, mostly. Two jugs for her milk. New cheese cloths for squeezing the curds. I fill the first bag.

"I'll take that," Court says, and I walk the six or so steps to hand him the full one.

Matilda sniffs at it, then resumes eating the grass around one of the poles.

I arrive at a fudge booth, and the smell of chocolate is so sweet and tempting, I have to pick up a sample. The creamy smoothness makes me want to swoon." You should try this!" I tell Court.

He ties Matilda to the pole and comes closer. "What have we got here?"

"Made with cream from our own herd," the woman says proudly, cutting a few more samples to put on the tray. "Try the chocolate caramel."

Court holds up his hand. "I'm hay and goat hair covered."

I pick up the tiny square sample. "I've got you."

He opens his mouth, and I feed him the bit of fudge. My fingers brush his lips, and everything in me ignites.

Our eyes meet, and his expression shifts from easy to intense, sending another flash of heat through my body.

So much time passes that the woman clears her throat. "Is it okay?"

We shake loose of whatever we might be feeling.

"Exceptional," Court says. "We'll need six pounds of that."

I turn away from him, almost sad the spell is broken. "You won't be able to roll us out of your apartment if we eat all that."

"Apartment?" the woman asks. "Where do you put your goat?"

This shifts the mood again. Court and I glance at each other conspiratorially and try not to laugh.

"We'll take a half-pound of the caramel fudge and a half-pound of plain chocolate," I tell her.

"Sounds good for me," Court says. "What are you getting for yourself?"

I giggle again. "Okay, add a half-pound of the s'mores fudge."

"There's s'mores fudge?" Court's eyes light up.

I feed him a taster. He groans. "Make it a pound."

The woman happily cuts, weighs, and wraps the three rectangles. "Here you go."

I tuck them in another bag and check on Matilda as Court takes the credit card from me to pay. She's found a bush near the end of her tether and is happily munching.

"We can look at a few booths together," I tell Court. "Matilda is occupied and in easy sight distance."

"All right, then." He takes my arm and tucks it in the crook of his elbow, like we're walking through a county fair in a movie starring Judy Garland or Dick Van Dyke.

It's magical and lovely, and I refuse to feel any concern about what it does or doesn't mean.

Or how my heart catches.

## 24

## COURT

The day feels short. We fill up Lucy's four bags and go back to buy two more.

She gets more starter culture for her goat cheese and two types of seasonings to expand her offerings.

We find a hand-painted milking stool that makes her smile, so I buy that, too.

By the time we get back to the SUV, everyone is tired, even the goat.

The sky is darkening as we head toward the highway.

"I know we just ate our way through all those booths, but I could use a milkshake," Lucy says.

"Your wish is my command," I say, punching the restaurant button on the map app built into the SUV. "There's a Checkers ahead."

"What's Checkers?" She rests her head on the back of her seat.

"Fast food burgers and shakes."

"Sounds perfect. Fast-food places have the best shakes."

"Not worried about chemicals?"

"Some days you need a little artificial flavor."

I swing into the drive through. "Chocolate? Vanilla? Strawberry?"

"Yes," she says.

I chuckle and order all three. "Fries with that?"

"Yes."

"Cheeseburger?"

She laughs. "Nice try."

We pull up to the delivery window to wait. The sky is bright with colors. "Is it hard to see the sunset in Manhattan with all the tall buildings?" she asks.

"Not if you're high enough."

"I see. So, if you're able to get to the top of a building, then you get to see sunset." She yawns.

"That's right." I pass her the first shake and set the other two in the center console, then balance the packet of fries between them.

I half-expect the goat to protest she's not getting anything, but when I check my rear-view mirror, she's lying down in the hay we spread. Both girls are settled.

The highway is quiet as we drive back. It's peaceful and easy, Lucy munching french fries beside me, sipping from each of the three shakes as she goes.

"You have to try the strawberry," she says, holding the straw close to my mouth.

I snatch it between my lips. The shake is icy cold and sweet, not artificial tasting at all. "It's good."

"It is."

She turns on the radio, and I expect to hear country or folk come out, but she settles on a top hits station. "They better play some Taylor, or I'll call in until they do." She settles down in her seat, resting the cup on her belly.

"What's your favorite Taylor song?"

"Oh, that's hard." She takes a sip as she thinks. "*Shake It Off* is my mantra, and I sing that one a lot. But probably not my favorite."

I wonder what she's needed to shake off, other than her parents. That man from college? People who make fun of her lifestyle?

Did she have to shake *me* off after our first argument in my office?

But I say nothing, just let her think about it.

She eventually says, "I think it changes as I change."

"You've had a lot of favorites, then?"

"Sure. I'm younger than her, but she's been a force as long as I've been old enough to know what songs can do."

"What was the first one that mattered?"

"Oh, *You Belong to Me* for sure."

"You were a romantic. What were you, thirteen?"

"Twelve. Big year for figuring out your romance aesthetic."

"I was sixteen when that song hit."

"You remember your life when Taylor Swift songs came out?" She's amused.

I remember the song because of the girl I was dating at the time, but I decide not to say that. "I got my driver's license that year, and it played a lot on the radio."

"You were driving a car, and I was driving my parents nuts with my dietary demands. I spent summers with BeeBee. Grandpa had died the year before, and she liked the company."

"Did you have a lot of cousins competing for her?"

"No, my dad is an only child. My brother and I were the only grandchildren."

"Your brother didn't have the same attachment?"

"No. Jasper was a video game playing thrill seeker. Spending hours weeding radishes wasn't his idea of a good time. He hated Taylor Swift."

I can picture her, young, kneeling in a garden next to the older version of her, carefully tending plants.

"But you never outgrew her music."

She switches out her milkshakes. "Nope. When *1989* came out, my top song switched to *Wildest Dreams*. That might still be my favorite."

"You like romantic yearning."

She smiles around her straw. "That's Taylor Swift in a nutshell."

Lucy doesn't strike me as a dreamer. She's so practical with her knapsack and bare essentials.

"Do you do art yourself?" I ask. "Paint? Write? Sing? Dance?"

"Not really. BeeBee always felt art was in nature. A new seedling unfurling from the ground. The perfect curl of a yellow squash."

"I like that."

Headlights flash around us. We're approaching the

island again. The car is so cozy, and the conversation so easy, I'm tempted to find a circuitous route so we can stay on the highway longer. It won't be the same once we're dodging taxis and waiting on pedestrians in the city.

Lucy settles against the headrest. She must be exhausted. Everything I've understood about pregnancy is how tiring it can be. It must take a lot of energy, growing a human.

Will it be mine? She keeps insisting it's true. And the more I get to know her, the more it seems like she wouldn't come all this way if it weren't.

In the end, the route doesn't matter. She's asleep by the time we get back to the building. I sit in the parked car, wondering if there's an easier way to get the goat up to the apartment.

I touch her shoulder. "We're here."

She startles awake. "Oh, time to be stealthy."

But we encounter no one in the halls or the stairs, and this time, there are no wild dashes. Lucy leads Matilda into the elevator while I carry the bags. The goat is more docile when she's tired.

When we make it inside my apartment, I tell her I'll fetch the bales of hay.

"Just get the one," she says. "We might be gone before we even get to the second one."

Right. Devin is supposedly booking her a farm again.

When I return a second time with the hay, the goat is asleep under the mist. I take the bale out and spread part of it around in case she wants to use it as bedding.

I slow down as I pass the guest room. The door is open, and I half-expect to see Lucy asleep already. But the shower is running in the adjoining bathroom.

I head to the kitchen and find she's already put away the jams and fudge and other items we've bought. The recycled bags are folded and placed on a shelf in the pantry.

My footsteps are slow as I pass her room again. She's still showering.

Not a bad idea. The sun and dust and general wandering outdoors have made me feel gritty.

I take a quick shower and change into cotton shorts and a T-shirt. When I return to the kitchen, Lucy is there, pouring a glass of milk.

Her hair is damp and wavy, making the pink T-shirt we bought this morning dark on her shoulders. She likes sleeping in her yoga shorts, and the shiny black material molds to her thighs.

"You feeling okay?" I ask as I fill a glass from the fridge dispenser.

"Much better now that I'm clean." She sets down her glass. "Oh, I got you something!"

"You did?"

She enters the pantry and returns with a small box. "I hid it in there."

"You were sneaky."

"It's just a little something."

I open the lid. Inside is an enamel keychain. I lift it out. It says, "Best goat dad."

"You've been so terrific with Matilda. You made a home for her! And you sneaked her into your apartment in spite of the risk. You let her come with us to the expo." She presses her lips together, and I can see she's trying to hold back her emotion. "You were made to be a dad. You're going to be great at it."

I know I should simply thank her for the gift and move on.

But I don't do that. I reach for her, tucking a strand of wet hair behind her ear.

When she looks up at me with those misty eyes, emotional, raw, I feel it all mirrored inside me. And I know I'm going to kiss her. I know we're going to do more.

It feels inevitable.

And right.

## 25

## LUCY

I know Court is going to kiss me a split second before he does it.

My body sinks into him as his lips brush against mine.

For a second, I think, that's all it's going to be. A gentle, friendly gesture.

But then he pulls me against him, and there's nothing soft about it.

My body buzzes as we connect, all the round parts of me pressing into the wall of him. He cups the back of my neck and draws my face more tightly to him. His tongue parts my lips.

I'm falling into him, like he's the cool river I need to dip into after a long, exhausting trek through hardship.

And he is. Everything that was a struggle is easy now. Food. Shelter. Care.

Court Armstrong isn't salty at all. He's perfect.

Memories of him from eight months ago flood

through me as he wraps his arms around my waist. His mouth is warm and demanding, and every few seconds, the ground seems to move beneath my feet on his kitchen tile.

This kiss goes on and on, sending showers of anticipation arcing through me. His fingers find the base of my shirt and slip beneath it, sliding up my back.

I was prepping for bed, so I didn't put on a bra. There's nothing to get in the way of his tender exploration.

My skin tingles in the wake of his touch. He wanders upward until the shirt is pulled tight on my belly and stops his progress. He moves his hand down and around, slipping the fabric up as he goes.

Cool air hits the base of my belly and inches its way up. My mind gets distracted by visions of my pale, stretched skin being so visible in the harsh overhead light. I press my hands on top of his.

He stops immediately. "I'm sorry. Of course."

I squeeze his fingers. "Can we go to some other room?"

Relief floods his features. "Absolutely."

He takes my hand and leads me down the hall, past my guest room, to his.

We enter without turning on the lights, the dim glow of the hall leaving soft shadows across the floor and bed.

He turns to me and draws me in for another kiss.

My senses are heightened without the worry over the lights. His beard is a tickle against my cheek and chin and nose. His mouth is warm and minty.

I shiver when his hands return to the bottom of the T-shirt and slowly lift it. The hem slides along my skin like a caress, over the curve of my belly, at the base of my breasts, then slipping across my nipples.

I suck in against Court's mouth, trying to suppress a cry. Everything is more intense than I ever remember. The pressure of his mouth. The air on my skin. The moment of release when the shirt lifts free of my body.

So much of me is bare, the breeze of a ceiling fan brushing against my cheeks, my shoulders, the tips of my breasts.

Court doesn't return to the kiss but presses his mouth against my neck, my collarbone, and down to the sensitive swells. He lifts them both and captures one nipple, then the other in his mouth, gently, so gently, as if he understands how tender they are, how exquisitely delicate since I've been pregnant.

There's no way he can know, of course, unless he read about it when he was learning about pregnancy, but he seems to be tuned into me, attentive, knowing when to intensify and when to go lightly.

I flash with different needs every few seconds. Be fast and hard and intense. Be gentle and careful and good. I'm whirling, my head swimming, but Court's there, adjusting, understanding each grip of my hands on his shoulders, or when I go still.

How does he do it?

I can't think on the question, because I've squeezed his hard bicep, and he's responded by gripping my butt and dragging me against his hips, grinding me against the erection I know I've dreamed about in the months since New Year's Eve.

It feels too familiar to have only known once, as though my mind has mapped each inch in the time between. I lift a leg and prop my foot on the end of the bed, allowing more intense grinding right where I want it.

I'm so desperate for him. So needy. I squeeze his arm again, and that's it, the yoga shorts are gone, leaving me in pale-green panties that fit below my belly.

He growls against my chest as his finger slides along the perimeter of the stretchy band. "I remember what you like," he says.

"You do?"

He scoops me up from the floor and places me on the bed. "I remember everything."

I press my hand to his cheek. Does he?

He slides a pillow beneath my head and kisses my mouth, the center of my chest, each breast, then skitters down my belly. For a moment, he presses both hands on the sides of the mound, then he whispers, "Hello in there."

A quick tear dashes down the side of my face that he's acknowledging the baby directly.

Then my mind is erased as the panties slide down. They hit the floor with a soft whisper, and he leans down between my legs, shifting them apart with strong, determined hands.

His beard tickles my thighs, then I can think of nothing else as his tongue slides against my skin, slipping inside.

I grasp the bedding with both hands, tilting my hips up. I can't see him, not even with the pillow under my head. My belly is too big. I think I will get uncomfortable in this position for too long, but then I don't think about anything but his hands spreading me wider, and his mouth hot against me.

My body ignites. Parts of me buzz again as my blood pounds, my head, the tips of my breasts, my fingertips. I'm more alive than I've ever felt.

Where he works me starts to tighten, gathering strength. I gasp, sucking in air, more tears coming. It's so intense and beautiful. I'm overwrought with emotion. It's Court. It's the baby. It's the three of us finding our way.

It's attention. It's closeness.

And it's peaking. I gasp and cry out, saying Court's name, spilling gibberish, the pulses heavy and intense. I see stars, like the sky has been revealed.

I'm high, so high, like I'm flying and happy and can't contain it all, not in this room, this building, this whole wide world. I want to reach down and hold his beautiful head, get him to come up to me, but I'm too big, and my hands won't reach.

But he knows, just as he's known everything this whole day. He takes my hands and kisses his way back up the globe of my belly, crawling over me.

"You have your shirt on!" I cry, snatching at it to pull it over his head.

"I was busy," he says, grinning over me as he tosses the shirt away from the bed.

I want to touch him, everything. Those muscled

shoulders, that honed chest, the tight belly. I can't get very far before I encounter the limit of my belly, so I shift to my side. He lands beside me on the bed, and now it's much easier. I can reach all of him, and I do, pushing his shorts out of the way until he's out and in my hands.

His head drops back as I reacquaint myself with him, long and hard and hot. I get familiar again with the length and breadth, the fat tip and thick veins.

"We don't have to penetrate if it makes you worry," he says, his voice gravelly.

"Are you kidding?" I say. "The one time I can't get pregnant. You bet I'm taking advantage of that!"

"Do you want me to wear a condom, anyway?"

I don't pause in my attention, but I think it over. "This would be a terrible time for an STD. How prolific have you been since New Year's?"

He hesitates, and I think it's because the number is so high. Yeah, condom it is.

But then he says, "I haven't, actually."

I let go of him and sit up. "What? Why?"

He props his head on his hand to face me. We lie side by side in the faint light. "I haven't been in a very good place since then. Since before then."

I run my hand down his arm, bumping along his muscles and the turn of his elbow. "Do you want to talk about it?"

He rolls onto his back and covers his face with one arm. "I don't do that."

There's a whiff of his salty self in the words, but I won't let him go there.

"Then let's not talk about it." I sit on my knees and drag his shorts down his legs. "Can the mother of your baby talk dirty, or would that ruin everything?"

His laugh is rumble. "I think it's incredibly hot."

I straddle him and lean down until I'm inches from his face, my belly pressing against his. "Then shut your damn mouth and *fuck me*."

## 26

## COURT

Fuuuuuuck. Those words coming out of sweet farmgirl, big-bellied Lucy almost make me shoot my load. My whole body shakes for a second, and she laughs. Laughs!

"You're so easy, Court Armstrong. Sit back while I have my way with you."

And then she's on me, sliding down my shaft until our bodies rest against each other. I'm deep inside her.

Fuuuuuuuuck.

Looking up at her is like a dream. Her honey-brown hair falls forward, all dry and curling on the ends. Her breasts loom over me in a temptation I absolutely cannot resist, so I lift up in an ab crunch to take one in my mouth.

But I fall back only moments later, when she rises over me and slides back down in exquisite, maddening slowness.

Her arms are propped on the pillow on either side

of my head. Her belly rests on mine no matter where she is in the rise and fall of her hips.

I figure it's best to let her set this pace since I don't know what's comfortable for her this late in her pregnancy.

She closes her eyes, a content smile on her lips. She's happy here.

Then something in her catches, and she moves faster. I hold her on each side of her ribs, helping take the weight off her arms.

"Oh, God, oh yes," she says, and I steel myself against the rising tide of pleasure to make sure she gets everything she wants out of this ride and more.

Her body heaves as she moves up and down, then side to side.

"Court!" Her voice is raspy as she lets herself go, tightening around me.

I'm with her now, lifting to meet her movements. Her body clamps down, over and over again, and that's it. I'm losing it, pulsing into her as my vision goes starry, and the figure of her is bathed in an ethereal glow.

She holds still, letting me fill her. Then her arms collapse, and she's on me, more or less, her belly keeping her farther than I think she'd like.

Even so, her forehead rests on my chest just under my chin. We breathe together, our inhalations the only sound in the room.

I run my hands up her back and gather her hair.

Then I feel the oddest thing against my stomach.

A twitch.

A thump.

Is that…

Lucy looks up. "We woke him up."

"Is he kicking?"

She laughs. "He is. Right in the gut."

I hold still, waiting for it to happen again.

Then it does.

*Thump.*

He's real. He's an actual little person with a leg and a foot.

And apparently, opinions about our activity and position.

"Yeah, I have to move," Lucy says, carefully sliding off my body to the bed and rolling to her side.

We face each other. I rest my palm on her belly. Would he stop kicking now that she's changed positions?

But no, there it is again. *Thump.*

"Does it hurt when he does that?"

"No. It's weird, like I have an alien in there."

"I bet."

"It's wildest when I'm lying perfectly still, and yet, my body moves."

"Can he hear you talking?"

"Oh, absolutely. I wake him up all the time if I call to Matilda. I'm sure it sounds muffled, like when you go underwater. But it's been proven they can hear. They recognize their mother's voice when they're born."

"What about outside voices?"

"Those too. There are some schools of thought that they even know the steps you take to walk in your house.

The creak of the front door. The tinkle of a spoon stirring milk into your coffee. Your routines are their routines."

"That's remarkable."

"Talk to him enough in this last month, and he'll know you, too."

Would he?

"Hello, baby," I say.

She runs her hands along the skin of her belly. "I guess we should wait on the test to talk about names."

"Do you have any in mind?"

"Mildred or Agatha, if she's a girl. Herman maybe, as a boy."

I sit up. "What century do you think this is?"

She laughs. "I'm kidding. I haven't thought too much about it. I guess I always refer to him in my mind as just 'baby.'"

"I guess you could name him the old-fashioned way."

She props her head up on her hand. "Family names?"

"Random name generators on the internet."

"You're so funny. I was named after my great-grandmother. Lucille Marie."

"I like it."

"What's your middle name?"

"Court Julian."

"Oooh, I like Julian."

"Really? I always wished it was my first name. Court got me lots of teasing."

"How?"

"Basketball court, courtesan, courtroom, courtyard."

"Is it short for anything?"

"Nope. I tried switching to Julian in middle school, but it didn't stick."

"I'm named after a mean cartoon character and a wacky sitcom."

I laugh. "But they're cool. Nobody messes with Lucy, either one."

"Kids are mean no matter what your name is."

"Also true."

She rests her head on the pillow. "Julian. Julian Brown. I'll have to fill out the form in the hospital. I don't know if we'll know in time to make him Armstrong."

That's a conundrum. "We'll figure it out."

She runs a hand along my arm. "Did the teasing as a kid bug you?"

I think she's still trying to get at what makes me salty. "It wasn't any worse than what everybody got."

"Did you always know you wanted to work in a New York business?"

We're heading into personal territory. "I don't know many kids who think to themselves, 'I want to work for a mid-sized media conglomerate when I grow up.'"

"Is that what Pickle Media is?"

"Yeah. It started as the marketing arm for the Pickle delis, then expanded."

"When did you take it over?"

"When I graduated with my MBA. The company

was always meant for me. Uncle Sherman likes to spin off companies for family."

"I see. Must be nice to know where you're headed and have a place ready for you."

"Or maybe it takes away all your choices."

She lifts her head. "Is that why you're so salty at work?"

I figured that was on her mind. "Who says I'm salty at work?"

She sits up, working the covers until they're loose enough for her to wrap them around herself. "Well, let's see. I bet Devin would say it. And probably Dawn from merchandizing. And I'm pretty sure I got tyrant vibes from everyone in the hall that day Matilda got loose."

I cross my arm over my face. "I have a reputation, sure."

"Deserved." She lifts my arm to make me look at her. "And yet, here you are, sweet as pulled taffy and just as flexible."

I don't respond to that. She waits awhile, then sighs and slides next to me, her head on my shoulder. "What do you do for fun?"

"Work out."

"What about all those well-loved carpentry books on your shelf?"

I go stock still. "You were snooping in my things?"

"Oh, there it is. Salty Court. There's nothing to snoop here. You could move in any family, and nothing would have to change."

I sigh to show my aggravation. "I don't spend much time here."

"Not even on the weekends?"

"I belong to a couple of informal sports leagues. It keeps me busy."

"I see. Did you skip out on them today?"

"It's fine."

"You did that for me?"

I stare at the ceiling. I'm not good at pillow talk. I prefer hotels where I can leave.

She bumps my chest. "Court! Bring back the man who was talking to the baby who kicked him in the gut while we were having sex."

She's right. My whole body has gone rigid and not the good parts.

She deserves something. We've changed the tenor of our relationship today. I know I initiated it, all of it. I have to follow through. "It was like you with your grandmother. I learned carpentry from my grandpa."

"Oh, that sounds lovely. Did you make things?"

"Everything. Tables. Chairs. Chests. Beds."

"What was the first thing you made?"

"A music box. We wired a spring inside, and it would play the *Blue Danube Waltz*."

"I bet it was lovely. Did you make it for your mother?"

"My grandmother. For Mother's Day."

She sighs. "Isn't it nice, the legacy family can leave us?"

I don't answer that. My legacy was shuttered with my grandfather's death. Uncle Sherman handed me a new one. I wasn't even out of high school when it was all decided.

I change the subject. "You think you might name the baby Julian?"

"I like it. And Julia, too. Maybe it's all set." She snuggles her head next to mine.

I draw her close. I'm glad she's content. It will have to be enough for both of us.

## 27

## LUCY

Life becomes a weird, happy dream.

Court and I decide Matilda is happy enough between her time in the apartment and on the balcony. He sets up a service to have a new shrub delivered every few days for her to eat, and we replace the diaper contraption's liners with proper compostable bags.

So, he tells Devin not to worry about finding another farm.

On Monday, Court goes to work. I take care of Matilda, milk her, and make goat cheese and soap. It's an easy walk to the spa to give it to Kaliyah.

I take Court a homemade lunch most days since the office is close enough to walk if I'm feeling good, or an inexpensive Uber if I'm feeling tired.

I get to know Joe and Penny from I.T. and Dawn from merchandizing. I take them cookies for their departments and make sure Court comes around and smiles once in a while. We organize a company pizza lunch for Friday, and I set to making dozens of cookies for the desserts.

Our nights are filled with leisurely dinners and long nights of learning all the ways a pregnant woman can comfortably have sex.

There are many.

I've never known anything like this.

When I'm home alone, I let April and Summer know things are going well. They're excited for me and glad Court is so much less salty than before.

I know it can last. I'm sure of it.

I hear from Stanley at his emporium, and he also places an order for goat cheese. He's uptown, so Court goes with me on Wednesday afternoon to deliver it.

His emporium is a glorified tourist trap near Times Square, full of kitschy objects like a bedazzled Statue of Liberty and foam fingers that read USA.

He sits behind the register in a funny red-striped apron with his emporium logo emblazoned on it. His face lights up when he sees me.

"Lucy and her goat! Where's your goat?"

We head to the counter. "She's in her happy place at the moment," I say, setting down the waxy paper package. "But I have her cheese!"

Stanley presses both hands on it. "Oooh, I can't wait to tear into this. When did you make it?"

"Milked her this morning and made the cheese a few hours ago."

He lets out a long sigh. "It doesn't get any fresher than that." Then he notices Court. "Is this the one you were headed toward on the subway that day?"

I glance at Court, who is sizing up the man with a sour expression I know well. I elbow him. "It is. We worked everything out."

Stanley accepts Court's glare with a beady-eyed stare of his own. "You take care of this young lady and her goat, or you'll hear from me."

Yikes. I'm not sure how Court will take that, but I'm surprised when he sticks out his hand in greeting. "I absolutely will, sir."

They shake. "He's all right by me, Lucy," Stanley says, releasing Court to turn to his register. It opens with a ringing chime. "And here you go for your cheese." He passes me cash. "I'll be asking for more, but you might be busy by then." He waves at my belly. "Whatcha got left? A couple weeks?"

"Eleven days until the due date. We have a sono-gram tomorrow." I take Court's hand. "We're going to confirm the gender."

"Happy days. I remember those. I got two kids. Jeb and Johnny." He thumbs at two young men in their early twenties, one sitting on a stool, and the other unpacking a box of New York commemorative spoons.

"They work for you!" I say, stealing a quick glance at Court to make sure he's not triggered by more evidence of family job expectations.

"Just till they finish college." Stanley sniffs in annoy-ance. "If I don't fire them for incompetence first."

I'm not sure how to respond to that, but I'm saved when the front door jingles and a flood of people come in.

"Four forty-five tour bus, right on the money,"

Stanley says. "Got to do shoplifting patrol. I'll be seeing you." He pulls a small stuffed bear with a red, white, and blue T-shirt out of the bin next to the register. "For the kid. Good luck."

I hold the teddy bear to my chest. "Thank you, Stanley." I know it's just a random bear from a tourist store, but it's the first gift I've been given specifically for the baby.

Outside, the sidewalk is thick with people headed home from work.

"Is it really only eleven days?" Court asks.

"Give or take a week," I say. "First babies are often late."

"You don't have anything. No clothes. No bottles. No diapers." He seems stunned, like he's putting all this information together in his head. "We should be assembling a crib, getting a swing. Do they still make swings? We'll need a high chair. And baby food. And those weird nubby things they put in their mouths."

I wrap my arms around one of his. "Hey, I'm simple. My baby will be simple. A few cloth diapers. Some onesies and soft blankets. I'll be breastfeeding, and that's all he'll need at first. I'll learn how to create a baby wrap from a long cloth. I bet I can even use a sheet."

He stops dead. "Is that how you want to parent? Minimally?"

"Why not? Millions of babies were born and raised without fancy rocking machines or sterilizers or designer all-terrain strollers."

"But don't those things make it easier?"

"I don't mind hard."

Two costumed buskers head for us to offer pictures, so I move him forward before we're mistaken for tourists. "But you're right. I should probably pick up a few basics. I have some money."

He stops again. "I have money."

"But we don't have the test yet. You want the test. I respect you wanting it."

He turns me to face him. "What if I want you, and the baby is extra?"

Does he? Can he know that?

I don't know that much about him, not how he ticks inside. Does he love hard and move on? Is he someone who can be counted on?

I peer up at him, a gusty breeze making his hair dance, his blue eyes penetrating me with his gaze.

I do know one thing. The baby is his, and we're in this together even if we don't work as a couple. "Okay," I say. "Let's get some things."

He digs out his phone. "There has to be a baby place somewhere around here."

There isn't, not in the hotbed of tourism, but we take an Uber in heavy traffic to another store that Court assures me uses natural fibers and a more eco-friendly approach.

When we arrive, the young woman at the register says, "We're closing in a half hour, but if you make your selections quickly, we can get you settled."

Court's face goes salty. I'm about to intervene when he slams his platinum card on the counter. "I'm having a baby in eleven days, and we need everything. Every single thing."

"Oh!" The woman glances at my belly, then back at him. "What do you mean, everything?"

I come around his side. "We've been overwhelmed since learning about the baby, and we haven't bought so much as a onesie. I think he wants to outfit as much as possible in one stop."

She glances around. "Okay, let me get some help." She walks to the door to twist the lock and switch the sign to closed. "Let's get started."

It takes three hours, the entire sales staff of four people, all who are getting bonuses for the extra time, and dinner ordered in for everyone to get it done. But we get clothes, diapers, baby wraps, blankets, burp cloths, baby toys, a bassinet, a changing table, a breast milk pump and all the accessories, and even nursing bras and tops for me.

We arrange for a delivery on Friday since Maggie will be there to clean and can receive it. I'll be helping with the luncheon that day, and we'll be gone tomorrow for the sonogram.

When did my days get so busy?

As we ride back to his apartment, my head on his shoulder, I ask, "Where are we going to put it all?"

"There's an extra bedroom."

"I haven't been in there."

He kisses the top of my head. "Why not?"

"It's been closed. I kept thinking you might have a sex dungeon."

He laughs. "I would have dragged you there by now, baby or no baby."

"That sounds like a way to induce labor."

"I had planned to create a workout room, but I like the one downstairs just fine, so I never did."

"So, it's empty?"

He hesitates. "Not exactly."

I sit up, my head flashing with thoughts about what could be in there. Keepsakes from old relationships? High school trophies? "What is it?"

"I'll show you."

We arrive at the building, and Jerry steps forward to open our doors. "Mr. Armstrong," he says. "And Lucy."

It's funny that Jerry knows me, but he doesn't know about our goat. "Good evening, Jerry. We're going to have another one soon." I pat my belly.

"I'll be here to bring the car around when it's time."

Court claps his shoulders. "You good in stressful situations, Jerry?"

"I've had fifty-two babies in this building while I was on duty."

Court takes a step back. "You're experienced!"

"Yes, sir."

Court takes my hand as we head to the elevator.

When we're inside, I ask, "Do you think he ever wonders where I was for the first eight months of this pregnancy?"

"Jerry makes no judgments," Court says. "I'm sure he's seen everything."

"We'll get a gender tomorrow," I tell him. "We'll know whether to call him Julian or Julia."

His brow pinches, and I wonder if he's thinking about how strange it will be to name a boy Julian if it's not his.

But he simply says, "Big day."

When we get inside his apartment, I check on Matilda, who is sleeping on her balcony.

"You want to see the room?" he asks.

"I do."

We head to the door. My heart hammers as he turns the knob.

When he flips on the light, I know exactly what I'm seeing. The room is serene in pale green. The bedposts are made of pine, intricately carved with vines of flowers up the poles. A matching dresser has flower drawer pulls and a mirror surrounded by a floral vine made entirely of wood.

On top of the dresser is a burnished, glossy box with inlaid woods in many different grains and color tones.

I walk up to it and open the lid, listening to the sounds of "Blue Danube Waltz" in a bright, tinkly tune.

"You made all this?" I ask.

"With my grandfather."

"It's beautiful."

He runs his hand along the dresser top. "It's out of fashion. The decorator wouldn't even work with it."

"I love it."

I hope this will be the baby's room. I can't say it right now. I couldn't deal with his doubt about paternity in this emotional moment.

And it's perfect. The day has been a dream. The whole week. And now, I get to see a part of Court no one else gets.

My yurt was enough. I was enough. I know that.

But this is more. This is safety. Security. It's a home.

# 28

## COURT

D evin stands in the doorway as I shut down my computer to leave. It's sonogram day, so I'm only working in the morning so I can pick Lucy up and drive out to the Warwick clinic.

We discussed moving to a New York doctor, but initial calls showed no one was accepting new patients, not even on a cash basis. So, we're staying with Warwick, knowing it's a risk if she goes into labor, and it's too intense to drive out of the city for the hospital where her OB/GYN delivers.

Devin retrieves a set of signed documents from my desk. "Lucy sure lights up the place. Everything is set up for the pizza party tomorrow."

"Good. Lucy's been baking all week."

"She's an energy ball, even this far along."

My mind flashes to last night and the things that happened on my grandfather's old bed. "She is."

"We look forward to finding out what you're having." He emphasizes the *you're* to make a point.

It's moot. I can't imagine sending Lucy away if the baby isn't mine, although we'd have to figure out how to handle the actual paternity.

I don't want to think about that. I want to have faith in what she says.

I tuck my phone in my pocket. "Hold down the fort for the afternoon."

"Not a problem."

It's pouring rain, so I grab a taxi back to the apartment.

Lucy's sitting on a stool by the stove, periodically turning on the oven light so she can check on a tray of cookies. Containers filled with everything from snicker-doodle to shortbread to chocolate chip cover the counters.

"Cutting it close on this batch?" I ask.

"They're about to come out." She shoves a hunk of hair from her forehead. She looks tired.

"Are you all right?"

"I didn't sleep well. Couldn't find a position that worked."

I rush over to her, running a thumb down her cheek. "What can we do? A new mattress? There were special pillows at that store."

She flashes a wan smile. "I think we're in the tough-ing-it-out portion of gestation."

I run my hand down her arm. "If you don't have enough cookies, we can buy the rest."

"I'm taking pride in making them all."

I make a rough count of what she already has. "It looks good already."

"We could use more macadamia nut."

"Then you'll direct me from a comfortable chair when we get back."

Another tired smile. "All right. That'll be something to see."

I wait until the timer dings and pull out the tray myself. Then I lead her to the bedroom to lie down while I change into more casual clothes for the visit.

"It's exciting, right?" she asks. "Knowing the gender for certain?"

"Now that the old methods have failed us?"

She giggles. "I can't get a confirmation from the stars. We'll have to use modern technology."

I hang up my suit and switch to jeans and a blue button-down to balance out Lucy's pink dress.

When I come out of the closet, Lucy is napping. I head to the kitchen to move the cooled cookies to a container, then check on Matilda.

She's standing by the railing, looking out at the rain. It's only a moderate sprinkle.

"You like wet skies?"

She turns to me with a short *meh eh.*

Her water looks good, and she has fresh hay.

"Be a good girl."

As if she's ready to prove she's anything but, she pushes her back end against the rails, lifts her tail, and poops off the end of the balcony.

"Matilda! No!" I rush forward to drag her more centrally onto the platform.

From far below, I hear, "What the hell? It's raining shit?"

I don't dare look down. I sit with Matilda, making sure she isn't visible from below. "That was not a good plan, Miss Goat."

She lowers her head. I know what's coming next, so I release her and hurry to the door before she can butt me.

When I slide it closed, she's glaring in my direction.

We're never going to be friends, it seems.

It's time to get going if I want to allow for bad weather. I head to the bedroom and stroke Lucy's hair. "Time to go, sleepyhead."

She stirs, then her eyes fly open. "Are we late?"

"A little early. I want to give us extra time since it's been raining."

"Oh! I need to check on Matilda."

"Already done." I take her hands and help her sit up.

She slides her feet into her shoes. "Thank you. I need to put those cookies away."

"Already done."

"Is the oven off?"

"I checked."

"Oh." She runs her hands through her hair. "Then I guess we're ready."

The rain slows us down on the island, but we come out of the Lincoln tunnel to bright skies.

We have to stop for Lucy to pee, which is becoming wildly frequent.

"You sure nothing's wrong?" I ask as she dashes back into the car.

"I think he's head-butting my bladder."

"The goat tried butting me again on the balcony today?"

"What did you do?"

I laugh. "Whatever it is, it's my fault?"

She takes my hand. "She's my baby. My first baby."

I get that. I don't quite understand it, not when she's growing a human baby, but I respect her feelings about it.

"She pooped off the balcony. I noticed there's been less to clean up lately. I'm worried she's been doing it when we haven't noticed."

"Do you think anyone has guessed where it's coming from?"

"Not sure. At least we're far enough down the building from where Jerry stands that he won't put two and two together."

"You mean doo and doo?"

I shake my head. This is my life now. Poop jokes.

Lucy is overcome with giggles. We pull into the parking lot of the clinic.

"Blood test first," she says, holding her belly. "I feel like I'm going to laugh the baby right out."

"Can excessive laughter cause you to go into labor?"

She's caught up in it again and can't answer.

I take her hand and lead my giggling lady up to the door. We're pointed to the lab.

She goes dead sober when the phlebotomist preps the needle. "Here we go."

"I thought you said you were fine with needles. I asked you last week when you made the appointment."

"I didn't want to seem like trouble."

"Do you faint with needles?" the phlebotomist asks. "This chair lies back to help you."

"I've come close, but I'm worried now that I'm so pregnant, it'll happen."

"Let me lay you back." She pulls a lever below the chair to lift a footrest and angle the back of the seat. "Dad, stay close to make sure she doesn't roll off."

"You're prepared for this," Lucy says.

"We have to be."

"Look at me," I tell Lucy and hold her gaze as the phlebotomist preps Lucy's arm. "What's your final guess on Julian or Julia?"

"Hmmm." She closes her eyes. "Julian." Then. "Ouch!"

"It will only take a few seconds," the phlebotomist says. "You're doing great."

"Then I'm Team Julia," I say.

"I like those names," the woman says. "And… we're all done." A cotton ball and strip of tape goes on Lucy's arm. "We'll sit her up slowly."

"I'm good," Lucy says. "Whew."

We take our time walking to radiology. I hold Lucy's hand tightly as we're checked in, and we wait for our turn.

"I don't know why I'm so nervous," Lucy says. "I'm fine either way."

"Probably you're ramped up from the blood draw."

She nods. "I'm going to need another milkshake or three."

I kiss her knuckles. "Anything you want."

We're called back, and a tall woman ushers us into a

dimly lit room. "Let's take a peek at baby!" She helps Lucy onto the exam table and covers her lower half with a paper sheet.

"Oh, I shouldn't have worn a dress!" Lucy says.

"Not a problem. I'm Olivia. Do you know your gender?" She rolls Lucy's dress up to her chest.

"Not yet."

"Do you want to know?"

"Yes," Lucy says. "Today's the day."

"I love these days." She squirts gel on a paddle and runs it over Lucy's belly.

I watch the confusing screen of black and white dots, unable to make out anything.

"Here's the head," Olivia says. She clicks on a few things. "Measuring perfectly." She shifts the paddle and clicks more. "Femur good. Might be tall like Dad. Let me measure a few other little things and see if we can get a look at girl or boy parts. Oh, let me turn on the sound."

She turns a dial, and that familiar *whomp, whomp* fills the room.

I lift my phone and record Olivia and her screen, then the glow on Lucy's expectant face.

"Everything looks perfect. Let me rummage around here." Olivia moves the paddle. "Ah, here we go."

I set down the phone and peer more closely. "What is that?"

"That's a penis," she says. "It's a boy."

My throat instantly tightens. A boy. All the images come roaring forward. Running in the park. Flying a kite. Throwing a ball. Racing across a yard.

I find Lucy's hand.

"Julian," she breathes.

I don't remember the last time I cried. Middle school, I think, when I broke my arm.

But it's happening. I'm overwhelmed. I see myself with my father, jumping in the car for a ball game.

Then, me with my grandfather. I can picture his eyes on me, his smile after I finished my first hand-made music box.

I get to be that person now. I may have lost him, but now I get the chance to *become* him.

The tears gather enough to fall, and Lucy squeezes my fingers.

I didn't know happy crying was something I could even do.

## 29

## LUCY

I'm floating on air Friday morning as I pack the last batches of cookies to take to Court's office for the pizza party.

We met Dr. Henry after the sonogram, and he assured us that if we didn't feel comfortable making the drive out to Warwick, he had associates at six of the Manhattan birthing centers. Just call his office or the after-hours on-call, and they would direct us where to go.

The front door opens, and a woman calls out, "Hello, hello! Where is the goat?"

"On the balcony!" I reply and head to the front door.

Maggie is a late-fifties woman with stenciled-in eyebrows, a helmet of senna-red hair, and the warmest smile I've seen so far in New York. "You must be Lucy. Oh, you are about to pop!"

I run my hands over the white shirt self-consciously. "A week or so to go."

"First baby?"

"Yes."

"You have time." She props the door open wide to push in a cart covered in cleaning supplies and bags of groceries. "I have food. I will clean. It's been two weeks. But Mr. Court is so clean." She sniffs the air. "You cook!"

"I'm making cookies for Court's office. We're having a pizza party there today."

"How delightful. So good for such a stern man." She closes the front door. "Now let me see that goat."

I lead her to the balcony, where Matilda lies in her hay.

"She is so small!" Maggie presses her hands to the glass. "She seemed bigger when she was running at me. Does she butt things with her head?"

"Only Court when he deserves it."

The woman's laugh is hearty and deep. "I like you, Lucy."

"I like you too. And don't worry about the balcony. That's my job to keep clean."

"Good. The goat scares me. But maybe we'll become friends." She heads back to her cart. "I hear all the baby goodies will arrive today."

"Yes, around eleven. Have them load it all into the green bedroom."

"Oh yes, that's perfect for the baby. So cozy." She pushes her cart to the kitchen. "I will unload and get out of your way." She spots all the cookies. "That's a lot! You take my cart when you go."

"Court is sending someone to fetch these. But thank you!"

"He thinks of everything."

I've barely packed the last box when there's another knock. That must be the courier.

I open the door to a young man with a handcart. "I'm here to take boxes to Pickle Media."

"Yes, in here."

I fuss over the cardboard boxes lined with parchment paper, making sure they're secure. I can't have them fall and all the cookies break.

I'm so excited. I've never done anything like this, and I feel like this could be the start of some genuine friendships in Court's office, not the least of which will be for him.

"Am I riding with you or going separately?" I ask the young man.

"You can come with me."

"Oh, good." I shove my phone in the pocket of my dress. "See you later, Maggie!"

The ride is short, and soon, the cookies and I are both safely delivered to the large conference room down the hall from Court's office. The big table has been pushed to the back wall, and the seats line the walls.

Dawn from merchandizing is there with a giant box. "Hey, Lucy! Devin, where should I put these?"

"Line them up by the plates," he says. "Cookies on the other end. I left you some trays."

Dawn and I both start unloading.

"What do you have?" I ask her.

"Court ordered these. Thought the motto could use an adjustment."

"From Dill with It?" I still have my water bottles.

"Look at them." She passes me a large cup with a built-in straw. It reads, "You can't DILL with my awesome."

"That's so terrible, it's good," I say.

"I know, right!" She lines the cups up along the wall. "Everyone gets one today."

"How fun." I tug a pair of plastic serving gloves from a box on the table and unload cookies onto plates.

I'm in the zone, arranging them by flavor, when I feel arms come around me. "I want to eat this right now," Court whispers in my ear.

I lift a snickerdoodle. "I can stuff it in your mouth."

He laughs, then coughs when I do, in fact, stuff a cookie between his lips. He takes a bite. "Almost as sweet."

"Court!" I elbow him.

Devin and Dawn exchange a glance at us, but they're smiling.

The pizza delivery arrives, and preparation begins in earnest. Two women from HR arrive to set up lemonade, tea, and water.

Within minutes, the first hungry employees poke their heads in the door.

"Come in," Court says. "Grab a bottle, fill it with the drink of your choices, and get pizza and cookies. Lucy did all the cookie baking."

He's making a point of mentioning me.

My belly buzzes with happiness.

More employees file in. The chairs fill up, and others stand around. Only a few grab their lunch and go.

Conversation flows through the room. I meet more employees. Court knows everyone's name, which seems to surprise some of them.

When we get a quiet moment, I ask him, "Did you learn everyone's names for this?"

He slides another piece of pizza from a box to his plate. "I did."

We make another round of chatting. There's no sign of the distant, off-putting boss I met my first day. People are talking about it, sending furtive glances as they gossip.

Court lifts his hands. "Hello, everyone."

People realize he's speaking and quiet down.

"I wanted to do a quick thank you to several key people who made this lunch happen." He gestures toward Devin. "My trusty sidekick Devin, who ordered the pizzas and got the room ready."

Everyone claps.

"Dawn in merchandizing who got us these cool and clever bottles." He holds his up.

There's some cheering and many toasts with the new bottles.

"Mimi and Jean in HR who got us drinks and helped decorate."

Another roar of approval.

"And most of all, to Lucy, who baked cookies for everyone and came up with the idea in the first place."

There's a huge round of applause.

My face gets hot with the attention, but I give a little wave.

"As a token of my appreciation, and I'm sure all of yours, I wanted to give her something." He pulls out a small box.

The roars get excited, and my blood pressure skyrockets. Surely, he won't propose at a party. We've only known each other for two weeks.

What will I say if he does? Do I do that? If Court wants to secure our relationship before the baby, does that mean he believes me? Should we give it a really hard try?

But he doesn't get down on one knee, and he doesn't open the box. He simply passes it to me. I notice the words "Natural Outfitters" on top. Clearly, they don't do engagement rings.

I'm not sure how to feel. Relieved? Disappointed?

I set down my plate to open the box.

The excitement has come down now that the gift is in my hands. Everyone realizes they misjudged the moment. Future grooms don't hand over a box.

Even Court seems to understand something else was expected and tugs at his collar.

I open the top. Inside is a heart-shaped locket with a goat on the front. "It's a goat necklace!" I exclaim. "Court has no hard feelings for how many times Matilda butted him with her head!"

This saves the moment. Everyone roars with laughter. I unclasp the necklace and put it around my neck. It's a difficult reach, but Court doesn't step forward to help.

When I continue to struggle to get it clasped, Dawn swoops in to assist.

While she's close to me, she whispers, "I'm sorry."

What is she sorry for? That we all thought he was proposing?

"I'm fine," I tell her. "I haven't known him long."

She squeezes my shoulders. "He'll figure it out."

The air seems to have been let out of the party, and it slowly dwindles until there's only me, Devin, Court, and the HR ladies.

"I'll put the extra cookies in the breakroom," I say, glad for an excuse to escape everyone.

I combine the leftover cookies into one box and carry it down the hall. I'm getting emotional, when I promised myself I wouldn't.

It was totally silly to think what I did. For all of us to think it. Court was the only sane one in the room.

But even so, it was a lot of excitement for a big letdown.

I'll be all right. We have a DNA test to do. By then, a couple more weeks will have passed, and we'll be tested in the most intense way by caring for a newborn.

We'll know more about our future as a couple when life get hard than we can ever figure out while things are easy.

## 30

## COURT

T he ride home on Friday is quiet.

I'm aware that I made a tactical error in bringing a jewelry box to a party when I have a pregnant woman in my life.

Our big triumph feels like a disaster, even though nobody said anything to me about it. Not Devin. Not Lucy. No one.

But I know.

As if the world wants to kick us when we're down, we arrive at my apartment to an envelope taped to the door.

"What is that?" Lucy asks, her voice catching.

I pull out the notice.

*It has come to our attention that an animal on a balcony on the east side of the building is defecating onto the street below. Extreme action, including eviction, will be enacted if this situation is not remedied immediately.*

. . .

Lucy sucks in a breath. "We're caught."

"I don't think so. It's not addressed directly to us." I glance down the hall. The closest door on our side of the hall is a considerable distance, but I see a rectangle of white taped to it. "They're fishing for who it is. Probably every floor on this side got these."

"But it's just a matter of time, right? In Summer's apartment, it was in their lease that they could come in anytime they wanted for maintenance or emergency. They could do that and find her."

I open the door. "We'll simply install a more solid barrier so she can't push her butt behind the edge of the balcony. It will be all right."

Even as I try to reassure her, Lucy runs her necklace charm up and down the chain in a nervous gesture. When we're inside, she hurries to the balcony to check on the goat.

I head to the green bedroom to ensure that the baby items were delivered as expected.

The door is open, and when I flip on the light, I'm greeted with a mountain of boxes, packages, and clothing. Maggie has already started washing them, and a clean folded basket of onesies, blankets, and cloth diapers rests on the end of the bed.

Lucy comes up behind me.

"Everything okay on the balcony?" I ask.

"Yes. Matilda is sleeping."

"Our order came in."

"Oh! Look at it all!" She reaches in the basket to lift

one of the tiny garments to her nose. "They smell so good!"

"They probably won't for long."

Lucy grins and picks up a blanket to rub against her cheek. Her eyes grow wet. "He's really coming. He has a place to sleep. And things to wear."

"And a name."

She clutches a blanket to her chest. "And a name."

I want to say something about the snafu at lunch. The words are on my lips.

But Lucy beats me to it. "Can you believe everyone thought you would propose? We've only known each other for two weeks!"

"I should have given you the necklace in private."

Her hand flies to it. "It's lovely. I saw the words 'Natural Outfitters' on the box. Did you pick it up when we went shopping that day?"

"Actually, I got it when I bought the shoes."

Her eyes widen. "Back then? But you hated me that day!"

"I didn't hate you. I was just… blindsided."

She sets down the blanket and walks into my arms. "I was blindsided when I found out, too."

We stand there together, surrounded by the baby's things. It doesn't matter what everyone else thought. The important opinion is hers, and we're fine.

On Saturday morning, we tackle assembling the bassinet and baby swing. We keep the goat close by until we can fortify the balcony. Lucy has to stop her from eating the colorfully printed cardboard.

"Too many dyes, baby girl," she says. "I'll get a carrot in a minute."

When we've made a big enough dent for the day, we head to the living room to rest and go over the hospital plan. With only eight days until her due date, we are, as they say, in the "zone."

"Come, Matilda," Lucy says, patting the sofa beside her.

But the goat circles the coffee table, lifting and lowering her head like she's upset.

Lucy sits up. "What's wrong, baby girl?"

Matilda prances back and forth, so Lucy gets closer. "Are you hungry? Need more forage?" She turns to me. "Is there a shrub out there, or did she finish it off?"

"Still half of one when I went out this morning. You want me to go check?"

"And we're sure it was a safe one? No boxwood or Chinaberry?"

"It's the same kind we had delivered a few days ago. They've been good about sticking to the approved list."

Lucy reaches out her hand to stroke the goat's head, but Matilda backs up. She races around the coffee table and leaps onto the sofa.

I'm about to bail, not wanting my usual head-butting treatment, but Matilda sits right next to me and presses her nose under my arm.

"You think she finally likes me?" I ask. "You do like me, don't you, Matilda?"

"So, now she has a name!" Lucy says with a laugh.

"She does if she likes me." I pat her belly.

Lucy comes to pet her, but Matilda tenses and lowers her head.

"What's going on?" I ask. "Why is she acting like you're me?"

Now Lucy looks worried. "I've seen this behavior in BeeBee's goats. Let me feel her belly."

She reaches out, but Matilda lets out a low warning bellow.

"Matilda!" I say. "That's Lucy! Your mom!"

But Matilda is unfazed, snapping at Lucy each time she reaches for her.

"Let me get some carrots." Lucy heads to the kitchen and returns with an entire bunch. "Would you like a treat, Matilda?"

Matilda presses more tightly to me, as if Lucy is offering her poison.

"Here, you give them to her." Lucy passes the carrots to me.

I hold them in my lap, and Matilda immediately begins chomping on the ends.

Lucy sneaks up and presses her hands on the goat's belly. "Oh, no."

"Oh, no, what?"

"She's pregnant."

I almost jump up but catch myself before dislodging the goat.

"How?"

Lucy sits on the coffee table. "Probably at the farm. I let her wander. Maybe she found a roving uncut male."

"That place is the gift that keeps on giving. How did you know she was pregnant from her behavior?"

"It's a common trait in a female goat to completely flip their personality when the hormones hit." Her eyebrows draw together in concern. "I'm afraid our time here is limited."

Everything in me goes still. "What do you mean?"

"It's already been too long for Matilda to be on a balcony in the city. The building is on to us. And now she'll have a kid? We can't do this to her or her baby. They need space. The baby needs to learn to forage and jump on heights and protect itself."

"How long is a goat pregnant?"

"About twenty weeks."

That's a good amount of time. "We have five months to figure this out."

But Lucy shakes her head. "She needs better nutrition."

"We'll get her what she needs."

"She needs space. Outdoors. Room to run."

Bits of carrots fly out of Matilda's mouth as she chomps.

"Are you saying we have to leave here? That I have to give up my place for a goat?"

"So now she's just 'a goat' again? Now that she's pregnant and too much trouble?" Lucy's voice becomes high and strident.

Mine rises to match. "She dumped her loads off the edge of the balcony on purpose."

"She's adapting to her situation the only way she knows how!"

"She's an animal. She does what we say."

"She's not an animal! She's Matilda!" Lucy tugs on the goat's neck, but without a collar or lead, she can't make any headway on pulling her away from the carrots. Then she sucks in a breath and holds her belly.

My anger instantly drains. "Contractions?"

"No, it's the stupid belly pains. They never end! This ridiculousness never ends!"

I want to reach out for her, but Matilda is firmly ensconced on my lap. By the time I extricate myself from the carrots and the goat, Lucy has run to her old guest room and slammed the door.

Well, this is great. Just great.

# 31

## LUCY

I sleep through the early afternoon, but when I wake up, I don't feel much better.

I have messages from April and Summer, responses from the teary text I sent after I left Court and Matilda on the sofa. They hadn't responded right away, so I fell asleep.

I read over what I wrote.

*Me: Matilda's pregnant too! And the apartment building is looking for the illegal animal. Court could get evicted! I think I have to leave New York! I don't know what to do!*

*April: You would leave Court?*

*Summer: It's been like two weeks. They barely know each other. You do what's right for you.*

*April: Says the girl who eloped in Vegas after four weeks.*

*Summer: Touché.*

*April: She's going to have three mouths to feed!*

*Summer: There's nothing for two of them to eat in that concrete jungle!*

*April: There's parks.*

*Summer: There's poisonous plants. And rats.*

*April: Lucy?*

*Summer: Lucy?*

I hold my phone for a moment, trying to figure out what to say.

*Me: We had a fight.*

*April: What kind of fight?*

*Summer: Screaming? Yelling? DID THAT SALTY BASTARD LAY A HAND ON YOU?*

*Me: No, no. He thinks Matilda can stay here, and I know she can't. He doesn't want to give up his place. I think Matilda and I aren't worth it.*

*Summer: SALTY BASTARD.*

*April: Oh, honey. Are you sure? Go talk to him. Maybe he's upset too.*

*Summer: AND CARRY A BAT.*

*Me: Matilda likes him better, to boot.*

*Summer: Uggh, the pregnancy flip. Shoot. Will she let you touch her?*

*Me: She wouldn't earlier. I will try again.*

*Summer: Bring her an apple. She can't resist an apple.*

*Me: Let me see what's happening in the apartment.*

I quietly open the door and listen.

There are no sounds in the apartment.

I pass the open door of the green room, crowded with boxes and baby things.

I tiptoe to the living room, not sure what I'll find.

But no one's there.

Matilda's on the balcony. There's a new wire mesh liner attached to the railing to prevent anything from falling beyond the edge.

So that's what he's been up to.

I stand at the glass door, watching Matilda sleep. This is a real problem. She needs to forage, to get a variety of leaves and sticks and nutrients. She can't give birth here. And where could we find a vet for a goat in the city if there's an emergency? We need to be near farms, places with the support we might need.

I turn away and head to Court's bedroom. But when I get to his door, it's clear he isn't there.

Where did he go?

I head to my phone and realize there's a sticky note taped to the outside of the guest room door.

*Off to play basketball with my cousin.*

I text Summer and April.

*Me: He left to play basketball.*

*Summer: That salty bastard!*

*April: That's good. You both need a moment to think things over.*

*Summer: You should go home. What do your parents think about you shacking up with a salty bastard?*

*April: She doesn't talk to them.*

*Summer: Oh, right. Well, you should. They're grandparents! They'll help!*

*Me: I haven't talked to them in years. They scare me.*

*Summer: They were always so nice, though.*

*April: They sold her BeeBee's farm.*

*Summer: Can you forgive them? They have that huge plot of land, and it would be perfect for Matilda. Then you and Court can figure things out without all this pressure of the baby's birth and the goat's birth and the apartment. If he's still a salty bastard, you can collect the child support and send the kid to New York for a week every summer.*

*April: And come to France!*

*Summer: Or live it up in Vegas.*

I will do none of those things, especially calling my parents.

*Me: Thanks for the pep talk. I just want to sleep until the baby comes.*

*April: That sounds like depression, girl.*

*Summer: Baby blues.*

*April: We're worried about you.*

*Me: I'll be fine. I'm always fine. You know that.*

*Summer: We used to know it. But now you're in a big city where you only know a salty bastard, and you're having his baby.*

*April: Salty B has money, doesn't he? Will he use it against you?*

I go still. They're right. He clearly does. He lives here, plus he didn't blink at all the things we've bought.

Could he try to take the baby after the test?

Maybe I don't want to do the test.

Maybe I need to figure this thing out without him.

*Me: I'll think about all this. I'm feeling overloaded. Talk soon.*

*April: Keep us informed, baby girl.*

*Summer: Let us know if we need to bring a bat.*

I click off my phone screen and bury my face in the softly scented pillow.

Why did I ever come here?

Now I'm stuck.

## 32

## COURT

The glossy floor squeaks as I pivot to duck around Matt, who makes a wild jab at stealing the basketball as I drive toward the goal.

I spin to avoid my cousin Jason, who's blocking the guard to clear my path.

But the giant form of Caleb is too much for me to get around, so I make a quick bounce pass to Jason and let him sink the two-pointer.

"Match!" Jason calls, and we all smack each other's hands to conclude the game.

This is good. I've missed playing with the guys. Missed working out. Missed my life before a woman and her goat.

I sit on the bench, chugging water.

Jason drops in place beside me. "You blew us off last week. I half-expected to hear you'd run for the hills after Dad's 'Be a good pickle' speech."

"I took her to a farm expo last weekend."

He laughs. "You? With the tractors and livestock?"

I elbow him. "She wanted to go."

"So you're getting along."

"She's been staying with me."

"And it's going okay?"

I run my towel over my head. "It was. Until it wasn't."

Jason takes a long pull on his water before saying, "I imagine it's contentious. She's pregnant."

"It's her goat that's the problem."

"Right. Where is that thing, anyway?"

"On my balcony. We're borderline getting caught. I'm not sure what they'll do when they find it."

"And she won't part with it?"

"It's her kid. Literally. And now it's pregnant, too."

"What? Is there something in the water?"

I drape my towel over my bag. "It's a goddamn nightmare, that's what it is. We were doing fine, then it all went to hell."

"Give it time. Not that it will get better. A baby is a stress no matter what. You going to hire a nanny or something?"

"I'm waiting to see if it's even mine."

Jason's mouth tightens into a frown. "About that. You know you don't have to wait until it's born. They can test while she's pregnant."

"Right, but it's a big needle and amniotic fluid and all that."

He shakes his head. "Aunt Caprice didn't watch Dr. Phil? My mom did."

"God, no."

"Those women were always doing it to be revealed

on the show. It's just a blood test. No needle in the belly."

"But I googled it."

"Then you did a shit job."

I reach down and pull my phone out of my bag. It's true, I only read the headlines for the search results. It was a tense moment. And Lucy hadn't wanted to ask the doctor about it.

Why is that?

My stomach grows heavy as I click on search results and read entire articles. Fuck. Jason's right. You can do a simple blood test. And Lucy had a blood draw the other day. We could have done it right then.

But we didn't.

"Bro, you don't look good." Jason smacks my back. "You think she's delaying the test on purpose?"

"We bought all the baby stuff."

"Maybe that's all she wanted? A cash cow?"

"I don't care if she bilked me for that. But what would her end game be?"

"Maybe she's hoping you'll fall in love with her, no matter how the test comes out."

Shit.

"Hey." Jason's voice turns serious. "I'm not saying that's what's happening. Obviously, you're in the running based on the timeline. But maybe guard yourself. Use your head."

That's pretty much the opposite of what I've been doing.

"When are you headed back to Austin?"

Jason tosses his bottle in his bag. "I'm flying out

tonight. Ping me if you need anything. You've got backup here. Dad. Grammy."

"I know."

He gives me a salute as he heads out of the gym.

A new set of players enters the court, and I'm half-tempted to jump into their pickup game, but I don't. I gather my things and start walking.

It's five miles to the apartment. Normally, I'd grab a taxi, but today, I want the time to think.

As far as I can see, I've got three problems.

One, why didn't we do a blood test? That's a big one. If she's so sure, why didn't she look it all up and be ready to prove her case?

Two, what do we do about the goat? I have a lease for six more months. But more than that, where could we even put the damn thing? Nowhere in Manhattan. I can't imagine commuting from someplace like Warwick every day.

Three, what are we even going to be to each other? We seem to be making some sort of run at being a couple, but it's not going well. Not now. It's only been nine days since I rescued her from that farm. Nobody knows anything about anybody in nine days.

Except I do. I know she's more beloved at my work than I am. That she's an asset there.

She's fierce about the living things in her care.

She's independent. She found ways to make money under extreme circumstances.

She's doing all the trying.

I need to try harder.

It starts raining by the time I'm halfway home, but I keep walking. It feels right.

I'm drenched when I make it up to the apartment. I enter with trepidation, not sure what I'll find.

But Lucy is in the kitchen, stirring a creamy sauce on the stove.

Matilda is up on the dining table, glaring at her. She sees me and jumps down for pets.

I pat her head, not sure how to approach Lucy. "Hey."

She doesn't look up from the pot. "How was the game?"

Her tone sounds fine, but I'm not sure if that's a good sign or if she's hiding how she feels. "It was fine. I got drenched walking home."

She glances at me. "Oh, you are."

"I think I'll shower."

She doesn't respond to that.

I wait a moment, then turn to head for the hall.

Matilda follows me.

Great. There are a thousand things she can eat or destroy in my room while I shower.

Her hooves clatter on the wood floor. When we arrive, I try to close the door on her, but she bleats pathetically and bangs her head on the wood panel.

I jerk it open again, not wanting Lucy to think I'm upsetting her goat. "Shhh, shhhh. Come on, then."

She likes this new space and instantly jumps on the bed. Great.

I set my bag down and plug in my phone. The light in the room starts to vibrate oddly.

I turn to see Matilda eating the lampshade. "No, no!"

I must come at her too fast, because she startles and jumps to the floor, knocking the lamp over. It lands on the floor with a crash and goes out.

Now there are shattered lightbulb pieces everywhere.

"Over here, before you cut yourself," I call her to the bathroom.

She trots over happily. I lead her into the large white-tiled room and shut us both inside. What can she get into? I grab the rug and open the door again to toss it into the bedroom.

Towels. I roll them up and secure them in a cabinet.

When I turn around, she's found my Sonicare electric toothbrush and happily chomps on the bristles.

I won't be using that again.

I pull it from her mouth before she ingests any plastic.

Everything on the counter is in danger.

I pick up the trash can and sweep everything into it. Beard oil. Hand soap. A couple of decorative doodads. Then I shove the can under the sink.

That's better. Now there's only tile, cabinets, and towel racks.

The bathroom has both a garden tub and a walk-in shower framed in glass. There's no door to it, just an opening on the opposite end from the spray.

I lift Matilda into the tub and dribble the faucet. She immediately licks at it. I hope that will keep her busy for the fastest shower in history.

I turn on the water and shed my workout clothes,

storing them in a high cabinet before they become goat food.

But I'm only in the spray for a few seconds when I feel a nudge perilously close to my junk.

I open my eyes.

Matilda has jumped out of the tub and looks up at me, blinking in the fall of water.

This is weird.

There's a knock at the door. "Everything okay with Matilda? I heard a crash."

I lean through the gap in the shower wall. "She knocked over a lamp. Careful of the glass."

"Do you want me to get her?"

I look down at the goat. She peers up at me like I'm the greatest thing on earth.

"I don't think she'll come."

Lucy opens the door, her eyebrows lifting when she spots me and the goat in the shower. "This is not a sight I ever expected."

"Goat infidelity. Guilty."

Finally, she smiles. "Let me get some bribes."

Matilda and I wait, wet and, I guess, both naked, until Lucy returns with an apple and a lead.

Matilda hesitates, but the lure of the treat is too strong. Lucy pops the lead on her and uses the apple to walk her out of the bath.

I hope this means things are better between us.

## 33

---

## LUCY

Things don't go back to the way they were before our fight, not quite. Court and I spend Sunday arranging the baby's room and putting clothes away in the dresser.

There are signs that he's different. When I find a checklist online of baby items and realize we're missing many of them, he's more resigned than eager to place the order. It's completely different from how he acted at the store.

I ask him to play the video of the baby's sonogram, but the gleam isn't in his eye anymore when we watch it.

Finally, at dinner, I ask him if there's anything more than the problem with Matilda.

At first, he puts me off, stuffing his face with pasta rather than answer.

But I persist.

Eventually, he opens his phone to a website about paternity testing and slides it over to me.

I pick it up. "What's this?" But as I read, I get it.

There's a blood test you can take at any point. And I just did a blood draw.

"You think I'm trapping you without knowing the baby is yours." It's not a question. I slide the phone back.

He doesn't respond, but this time, he doesn't eat to avoid talking. He pushes his plate away.

I don't feel like food, either.

"Court, I didn't know about that test. I wish I had. We'd have the results by now, and none of this would be an issue between us."

His expression hardens, and I realize more damage has been done than I thought.

My voice cracks when I ask, "How can you be like this?"

Finally, he speaks. "I'm not *like* anything. I'm here. You're here. The goat's here. The baby's coming. Nothing will change between now and then."

"But *we've* changed!" I stand from my chair. "It was wonderful. And now it's not."

He sighs. "It's a tough situation."

I pick up my plate and turn away. I don't want to be next to him. "It was tough from the beginning."

"But then we got a goat notice. Then we realized we had two pregnancies in the house. And you insisted we had to leave."

He's right. I did do that.

"And then you found out about the blood test," I add.

"Look, we're going through a lot."

I open the pot I'm using to compost food waste and scrape my plate into it. "I know."

"We can't expect to be some perfect couple straight out of the gate. We barely know each other."

I don't want that to be true. I want to think that we *are* perfect. That the baby will have this beautiful family to be born into.

I knew it was impossible, but I still wanted it.

I should have gone to the library. I should have looked up paternity tests. I should have known what I was doing before I came to New York.

But I didn't. I showed up, goat in tow.

My impulsiveness is catching up to me. My desperation.

"So, that's it?" I ask. "We exist like this until the baby's born?"

He sighs. "I don't know how to fix all this. The goat. The apartment."

Other people commute, but probably to get to farmland, it's too far.

I came with problems. I came with impossibilities.

My messages with April and Summer keep popping into my head.

*Call your family. They'll help!*

*Salty bastard has money, doesn't he? Will he use it against you?*

I know how the test will come out, but I keep forgetting that he has to believe me for now. And that's been shaken.

I open the dishwasher to have something to do.

"Maggie will get those," Court says. "I've increased how often she comes to three times a week."

"I can do it."

"But very soon, it will get harder."

I can't stop him from bringing in Maggie. I should be grateful. I know it. But I feel like a leech. A lying leech with a baby, a goat, and a goat baby. Too many problems.

Not worth any of them.

I close the dishwasher. "I'm tired. I'm going to bed."

"Lucy…"

I keep walking.

Last night, I stayed in the guest room, so I go there again.

Matilda won't come with me, so I don't try to drag her with me or take her to the balcony. Court can handle her. Hopefully, she'll mellow out as the pregnancy progresses.

I change out of my shorts and top and into pajamas. Almost everything I own Court bought me. I'm not my own person anymore. Even my goat loves him more.

I text with April for a while, feeling sick. She soothes me and says she and Summer went in on a gift for the baby. I type out Court's address for where to send it, even though I'm not completely sure I'll be here.

But where else would I go?

The baby shifts in my belly. He's coming soon, like it or not. Matilda's baby, too.

Some things can't be stopped.

When I come out for breakfast, Court is already gone to work. I make a piece of toast, not sure I can eat much more.

Matilda stands on the dining table, watching me warily. I guess Court let her in, or else she spent the night inside. She has her diaper on. I walk close to sniff it to see if she needs cleaning up.

She takes several steps away from me.

"Matilda, really? You're going to be like this?" The tears start. I can't control them at all anymore.

She doesn't smell bad, so that's one less thing to worry about at the moment.

I sit on a chair, and she skitters to the opposite side.

My fingers find the grooves of the deep scratches she's leaving in Court's table. He's been awfully tolerant.

I manage to swallow the toast and move to the baby's room, which brings me more peace. I set the bassinet to rocking, then the swing. I open and close the drawers, fingering the soft fabrics and letting the fresh scent of baby detergent waft out.

It will be okay. I'll be okay. Julian will be okay.

There's a knock at the front door. Is it Maggie? Court said she would be coming more often. I wait a moment, since she always lets herself in after knocking.

But there's only another knock.

I head down the hall and open the security panel screen to see who is out there.

And suck in a breath.

It's my parents!

How can this be?

How did they know where I was?

I smooth my hair and open the front door.

"Mom? Dad?"

Mom rushes forward to gather me in her arms. I remember this feeling, now that I have it again.

She was always a hugger.

Dad stands behind her. "Lucy-Lu," he says. "It's been so long."

Mom pulls back to look at my belly. "It's nearly time, isn't it?"

I don't know what to say. So many emotions roil through me that I can't contain them all. Shock. Rage. Relief. Hope?

"Can we come in?" Mom asks.

I take a step back.

Dad glances around. "Nice place. He's the dad?"

I shrug.

Mom can't stop staring at my belly. "You're carrying higher than I did. Are you feeling okay?"

"Mostly."

Mom walks to the sofa and sits down. "Please let's talk. I know you're very angry with us. I think we can find some common ground. Can we try?"

She sounds so reasonable.

I sit on a chair. When Dad enters the room, our attention is drawn to the dining room with a scrabbling sound.

It's Matilda, jumping down and racing for the living room, head down, aiming for us.

"Matilda! No!" I stand, but Matilda only butts the chair where I'm sitting.

When she spots Dad, she trots over, pressing her head into his hand like a puppy.

"So, this is the infamous Matilda," he says, rubbing her temple. "Mom always had goats like this around."

"Until you sold her farm to a developer."

He lets out a long rush of air and sits next to Mom. Matilda follows him and stands by his legs for more attention.

Mom straightens her skirt. "Let's clear this up right away. April and Summer felt this was probably the crux of your upset."

"You talked to them?" My body flashes hot.

"They contacted us," Mom says. "They were worried. They said things weren't on solid footing with the baby's father, and they wanted more people on your side."

"Like you were on my side about being vegetarian? Or loving the farm? Or being different from you all?"

Mom shares a pained glance with Dad. "We didn't do right by you on that. We kept thinking it was a phase. We should have gone to more trouble to cook for you."

"And maybe not sold the only thing I ever cared about?"

Dad leans forward, his elbows braced on his knees. "I know that farm meant a lot to you, but you aren't aware of what it meant to me. My father tried to force me there. To expand it and work in the sun, caring for animals I didn't love like they did. I wanted out of there.

They tried to trap me. When Mom was gone, I could finally eject that piece of my history."

I didn't know any of this. "But I wanted it."

"You were so bright, so smart. I thought I was saving you from yourself."

And look where I am, holed up in an apartment with a man who barely tolerates my lifestyle, same as them.

Out of the frying pan, into the fire.

"Will you let us help you?" Mom asks. "I promise we will respect your choices. Vegetarian. Composting. Low energy usage. Water conservation."

Would they?

"I won't leave without Matilda," I say.

Dad reaches down to pat her back. "We have the yard. I can shore up the fence. This is no place for a goat. I can't imagine this man of yours wants her here."

"She'll have lots of space to run," Mom says. "We can put you in your old room and make a nursery out of Jasper's. I was already thinking of retiring. I'll get out early. Help with the baby. You can even pursue a career again if you want. Or raise her at our house."

"Him."

They look at each other. "It's a boy?"

"Yes. Julian."

Mom clasps her hands together. "What a lovely name."

They're being so… reasonable. It has to be a ruse. A trap.

But I never knew Dad's story before.

"Lucy, we've had a lot of years to think about how we handled BeeBee's death," Dad says.

"You didn't think about me at all."

"We did," Mom says. "Just from our perspective. Not yours. We don't want to lose you forever. And we're thrilled to be grandparents. Do you love this man?"

I hesitate. How can I? "I don't know him that well."

Another glance between them. I know how it sounds.

"If you want to stay here, we'll figure out a way to be close," Mom says. "I can still retire. I don't think we can afford anything in Manhattan, but maybe we can rent a place in one of the boroughs. At least give you an out if it's not working with the father."

I can't tell them it already isn't.

"I still have the problem of Matilda," I say. "And she's going to have a kid herself in a few months."

"Oh," Mom says. "You really need a yard then."

"We found out about Matilda a few days ago…" I trail off. How did I get in this mess? It's embarrassing to have my parents know about it.

"We can help," Mom says. "We'll get Matilda back to Colorado."

"How?" I ask.

Dad strokes a preening Matilda. "We flew in, but we can rent a car and a U-Haul or a trailer for her."

Driving. That makes sense. I can't fly this late, anyway. "We've been getting SUVs with a big dog package in the back. It works well."

"See," Dad says. "We can make a family trip of it.

We'll call your mother's OB/GYN and make sure you can be seen. How much time do we have?"

"A week."

"A week!" Dad looks stricken. "We should go then. It will take two days to get home, maybe three. Annette, you can book some hotels once we're in the car. Plan for ten-hour driving days. We can't push Lucy or her goat."

"Is that okay?" Mom asks. "Do you want to come?"

And leave Court?

Isn't this what he suggested from the beginning? He told me to go home and have the baby and send him the test results.

I can do that. We tried my way, and it got too complicated.

Maybe there will be some other time for us. Later, when the baby is proven to be his, and Matilda's not pregnant, and we don't have to hide her on a balcony.

Right now, I'm tired. So tired.

"Okay," I say.

"Okay?" Mom's response is a half-sob.

"Okay," I repeat.

She jumps up from the sofa to wrap her arms around me, startling Matilda.

Dad stays with the goat, settling her back down.

"I'll help you pack your things," Mom says. "Bradley, find an SUV to rent one way to Colorado."

She wraps her arm around me as we walk to the guest room for me to pack up.

I almost hesitate as we pass the baby's room. It's set up.

But we can't take all that.

I get Mom started with packing my clothes in the guest room. Then I sneak to the baby's room to take a few onesies, a couple of the fancy ecofriendly diapers, and the teddy bear Stanley gave us.

I leave two things behind.

The goat locket. I'm still not sure what he meant by it.

And the phone. I'll get my own.

Court and I might have a moment in the future. But my little family needs a different home for now.

## 34

## COURT

I'm useless all day Monday. Devin sees it. The merch team sees it during our staff meeting.

Afterward, Dawn approaches. "Is everything okay with Lucy?"

I refuse to confess anything. "What makes you think anything's wrong?"

She waits until the other employees filter out of the room. "You don't look good. I know the Friday party had its... unexpected moments. And I thought maybe you and Lucy—"

"Well, you thought wrong. And maybe you should get your boss out of your thoughts all together." I snatch up my folder and quickly cross the room.

"Mr. Armstrong," Dawn calls. "You were better, and now you're not. If something's going wrong with Lucy, you should fix it before the baby comes."

I refuse to acknowledge her little speech. What-fuck-ing-ever.

When I'm back in my office, I fling the folder on my desk. It opens and papers scatter across the top, a few of them sailing through the room.

I'm reminded of the first day Lucy was here, when Matilda unexpectedly jumped on my desk. I scoot pages aside and find the scratches where her hooves dug in. My dining table looks about the same.

Offices and New York high rises are no places for a goat. But I have no solution for this. Devin looked into it, and there's a city ordinance against farm animals. Nobody can keep one permanently on the island.

The only way we can keep the goat for the long-term is to move outside of Manhattan.

I've got him searching for a place. See if there's anything that will work.

People commute from the boroughs all the time. I did it at first until I managed to rent this place. Real estate in Manhattan is hard to come by.

I hated every minute of that train ride. And to get far enough out to have a yard or green space would be even farther. I can't remote in or work from home. I'm the boss.

This is a crazy sacrifice for a damn goat.

Although, I guess, technically, it's for Lucy.

My head pounds. I head to the sidebar and pour a glass of chilled water. I don't know what to do. I want to believe her. I want happily ever after for all three of us. But I don't see how.

Devin knocks, then enters. "I have a list of rentals with spaces that could accommodate the goat and have a line in to the city. You're looking at a pretty incredible commute. You might consider keeping your apartment and getting a second place for the weekends."

"A cozy family two days a week?" I flip through the pages.

"Maybe better than none?"

"Maybe." He's right. These are far. It doesn't make any sense to try commuting every day. I could finish out the lease, then get something smaller in the city. See Lucy and the baby on weekends.

This sucks.

Devin holds up another file. "I got the report from the outside firm looking into company morale. They have several recommendations, from compensation restructuring to leadership retreats."

Right. I still have that problem. "Thanks."

Devin pauses by the door. "You can't ask her to give up her goat, you know."

"I know."

"But it's possible her priorities will rearrange once the baby is here."

"You think so?"

He shrugs. "Babies are kind of a big deal. She might be willing to board the goat somewhere once the family dynamic shifts."

"The goat is pregnant, too."

Devin's mouth makes a big "O" shape. Then he's gone.

I feel paralyzed by this problem. I can't hire a nanny in the city if she's going to work an hour away, God knows where. We have to figure this out.

I close my eyes and remember my grandfather's

shop. There was a fence in the yard where we would run with the dogs when the weather was nice. Grandpa would open the side door and let them run in and out of his workspace.

Once we even whittled the likeness of Banshee, a husky who loved to howl. Grandpa used it as the decorative top of a walking stick.

We could have had a goat there. She could run the fenced area. We could have expanded it. That's the thing about Colorado that Manhattan will never rival. All the open land. Mountains. Woods. Nature runs wild.

I consider texting Lucy several times during the day but end up putting my phone down, unsure what to say.

On the way home, I stop by the flower shop and grab a new bush for Matilda and flowers for Lucy. I've never bought her flowers. I'm smart enough to get live ones in a pot, not clipped ones. I'm sure she has feelings about that.

I practice opening lines in the elevator.

"Lucy, I have some options for us. Let's talk about them."

"Lucy, I think we can figure this out."

But when I make it inside, I instantly know something's wrong. There's an emptiness about the place.

I forget my rehearsed lines. "Lucy?" I set down the plants. "Lucy? Are you okay?"

Images of her on the floor, passed out, race through me. I run to the kitchen. The guest room. The baby room. My bedroom.

She's not here.

I circle back to the balcony.

Matilda is gone.

I turn to the kitchen. The Dutch oven I used for her water is cleaned and upturned on a dish towel to drain.

The compost pot is cleaned out, too.

I open the pantry. My groceries are there but not the spices and flavorings for her goat cheese.

I race to the guest room and open drawers. Her clothes are gone.

Shit, shit, shit!

I hurry to the baby's room.

Here, everything looks the same. The swing, the bassinet, the changing table. I open drawers. They might be slightly emptier, but I don't remember everything we bought.

Then I see her phone.

And the locket.

She left those.

I pick up the phone. The lock screen of Matilda is still active.

I don't know her passcode.

So, I have no way of reaching her. To figure out where she went.

She's just… gone.

I sit on the edge of the bed, the chain of the locket cool in my hand.

She left me.

Where could she have gone? Who would have taken her in?

She has less than a week until the baby is due.

I stand. Did she go into labor? Maybe left by ambulance?

Then I sit down again.

No, the goat is gone.

She took Matilda with her. She took the things she needed.

I wasn't one of them.

## 35

## LUCY

M y parents and I do a lot of talking on the long drive home.

Then we sing.

I had forgotten about that tradition.

We could be goofy, doing rounds of "Row, Row, Row Your Boat" and "My Bonnie Lies Over the Ocean."

Neither Matilda nor I can stay awake when Mom launches into her old lullabies.

I've made the right choice.

The ride is hard on me, and more than once, we pull into hospital parking lots when the belly pains feel like contractions. But when they settle down with water and rest, we move on.

I know my parents are serious about trying to mend things with me when they keep ordering veggie burgers on the route.

People can learn.

Could Court have?

We were too new, I remind myself. We don't have to be a couple to raise a baby. But New York isn't right for me, and it's time to face that we will never be in the same place. Court's family lives in Colorado, less than an hour from us, and I'm happy to let them be involved.

Maybe Court will visit them often, and Julian will know that side of his family.

It will be enough.

But despite all these pep talks, when we pull up to my childhood home, turn Matilda loose in the yard, and I finally climb into the narrow twin bed from my youth, I can't stop crying.

I weep myself to sleep, wake up weeping, and fall asleep again.

Mom checks on me and, worried I would get dehydrated and have contractions again, brings me water, juice, grapes, and anything she thinks will replace the fluids that refuse to stop leaking from my eyes.

But on the third day home, I finally come out of it. I get up and head to Jasper's room, where my parents have been working since we got back.

My parents sit on the floor, assembling a baby swing a lot like the one Court bought.

Dad looks up. "We got your old crib out of the attic. It wasn't quite up to the new standards, but I fixed it by adding more rails.

I run my hand along the pinewood crib. Every other rail is newer and carefully smoothed and varnished. Inside is a pale-yellow set of sheets and matching blanket. Strapped to one end is a faded plastic piano with fat keys I vaguely remember.

"Was that mine?" I ask.

"It was!" Mom says. "I didn't think it would work, but it does." She pulls herself up from the floor. "You loved to kick it with your feet and make sounds. You would laugh and laugh."

"There are pictures of that, aren't there?"

She nods. "That's probably why you remember it."

I push on one of the keys. A single bright note comes out. It strikes a chord deep within me, a core memory lost in the decades.

"You've done a lot of work."

Dad screws a metal bar onto the swing. "We decided to take off a few weeks, then your mom will go back to finish out her notice, and then I'll go back once she's home again. Once the baby room is done, I'll get started building a small shed for Matilda and her baby."

They're rearranging their lives for me, creating space for us. It's hard to trust that this is a good thing. The fear and resentment won't go away that easily. But they're trying.

Jasper's old bed is pushed in the corner, covered in a new neutral green spread.

Mom waves a hand on it. "We decided to keep it for whoever is doing the night shift. We ordered a rocker that should be delivered tomorrow, too."

"You didn't have to do all this."

Mom's face gets serious, and seeing her expression makes my eyes prick with emotion. "I think we do. We didn't see you for almost five years. We have to change. We have to fix this to deserve a place in your life. And Julian's."

I almost hug her, but I'm not quite ready to reach out yet. "Is Matilda okay?"

Dad looks up. "She's living it up in the yard. I won't have to mow again for a long while."

Mom walks over to the window to look down. "She ate all my roses, but we'll call it restitution."

"Oh, no! You loved those."

Mom shrugs. "I never tended them, anyway. Hired a man to come do it. She's saving me money."

I walk up beside her. Matilda stands in the shade on a milk crate Dad must have put out for her. She presides over the yard.

"She looks happy," I say. It's probably just as well we're not next to each other all day right now. She's still avoiding me. I'm hoping it wears off.

"She's doting on your dad, that's for sure," Mom says, turning back to the room. "I'd be jealous, except she's already knocked up by some other male."

We all laugh at that, and I think, *this is going to be okay.*

"Did you milk her?" I ask.

"Your dad did," Mom says. "Don't forget, he was raised with goats."

"I was!" Dad turns the swing upright and pushes the button. It moves smoothly back and forth.

"Look at that!" Mom says. "It's perfect."

"It makes a weird sound, doesn't it?" I ask.

"I don't think it's the swing," Dad says. He shuts it off.

The strange pitter-patter continues, and then I realize something's crawling on my ankles.

I look down.

No, my ankles are wet.

It's raining on my ankles.

Mom lets out a shriek. "Your water broke! Bradley, get the bag. We'll call the neighbors to feed the goat. Lucy, let's get you dried off and to the car. I'll call Dr. Fresno and tell him you're coming. I sure hoped we would make it to the appointment tomorrow so you could meet him, but here we are."

I feel stunned, and the tears fall all over again.

The baby's coming. Julian's coming.

And Court isn't here.

I left him.

I shouldn't have left him.

"Where's your phone, Mom?" I ask.

"In my bag. We'll call Dr. Fresno's office from the car."

"I want to tell Court." I'll have to look up his office number. I never memorized his personal number, and I left it in my old phone.

"We'll let him know," Mom says. "Let's get to the car."

By the time I change and load up, the first contraction has hit. Fear overwhelms me. This is happening. I'm having a baby.

I pant my way to the hospital. "Call Court," I tell Mom.

"Tell me his number," she says. "We'll get him told."

But I still don't know it.

"Pickles," I try to say.

"You want pickles?" Mom asks.

"No…" I grip the door handle, unable to say anything more as I ride out the pain.

"I ate so many pickles when I was pregnant with you," Mom says. "You can't eat until they assess you. But we'll get you some as soon as we can."

I want to correct her, to tell her no, he works at Pickle Media.

But every pain grips me with an unnatural terror. It's hard. And it hurts.

We arrive at the hospital, and Dad rushes around to my door to help me out.

I'm loaded into a wheelchair and taken to a room. It all happens quickly: the changing, the exams, the discussions, the plan. They call my original doctor, then the one in Warwick, then decide they don't need the records, really, as I'm progressing.

And then they give me an epidural, and all is well.

I'll just sleep right through this childbirth…

## 36

---

## COURT

At first, I try to find Lucy. Where could she have gone? Back to her yurt, somewhere, anywhere in Colorado?

I call the spa to see if she arranged for future goat milk. Kaliyah hasn't talked to her in a week. Stanley either.

On Tuesday, I stalk her old Facebook. I message her there, even though I know it's futile. She hasn't logged in for years and probably doesn't have a way to do it now.

Her old friend list is hidden, but I find comments from people named Summer and April on her account. These are the only friends she's mentioned. I write them, but they seem to have abandoned the platform, too.

I get on LinkedIn and find a chef with April's name, but I don't get a response there, either. Summer is nowhere and her full name, Summer Jones, is so common that I can't easily search for it.

Work is worse than ever. I have no desire to talk to

anyone, not even Devin. I insist he message from outside my office and leave me the fuck alone.

On Wednesday, Dawn shows up with samples of the new merch, and I have to control myself not to throw her out. She scurries away as fast as possible. I cancel all other in-person meetings for the week, then on Friday, I don't even bother to go in. Pickle Media can run without me.

The baby's room is making me crazy, so I start packing it all up to donate.

I'm in the middle of that when Rhett texts me.

*Rhett: The whole family is talking about you.*

*Court: Like I give fuck all.*

*Rhett: Go ahead and be your asshole self with me. I get it. But do you want help or not?*

*Court: What would you do exactly?*

*Rhett: I don't know. Did you hire an investigator to find her? Where do you think she went?*

*Court: No clue. I didn't jailbreak her phone, but she was talking to her two friends before she left. She said so.*

*Rhett: Where are they?*

*Court: Vegas and France.*

*Rhett: You check Vegas?*

*Court: Right. Because that's a town where it's easy to find people who want to be lost.*

*Rhett: But she has a goat. A goat in Vegas will stick out about as much as a goat in Manhattan. Check social media. People might have posted videos.*

*Court: It's useless.*

*Rhett: It's not like you to give up.*

*Court: Fuck off.*

*Rhett: Yeah, I get it. I totally get it.*

Does he? I doubt it.

I drag the swing to the living room. It looks ridiculous there, but at least it will be gone soon.

I unload drawers, but every stack of baby garments I pick up is a stab to my chest.

Maybe Maggie can do this. I just need to move the heavy stuff.

I start pushing the changing table into the hall when my cell phone rings on the dresser.

The caller ID reads *UNAVAILABLE*. I answer the call, my heart pounding. Could it be her? "This is Court."

"Court Armstrong?"

My shoulders drop as I realize it's not Lucy.

"Whatever you're selling, I don't want it."

I'm about to hang up when she rushes out the words, "It's the OB/GYN's office."

I lift the phone back to my ear. "Is Lucy okay?"

"That's what we wanted to ask you. We got a request for her records this morning, then a notice that she was in labor in a hospital in Denver, Colorado."

I make up a lie, so it seems I'm in the loop. "She's visiting her parents. Which hospital?"

She rattles off the name, and I race to the kitchen to grab something to use to write it down.

"Are you not with her?" the woman asks.

"I'm on the way." That's not a lie. "When did you get the call?"

"About two hours ago."

She could have had the baby by now. Or it might be twenty more hours. It's impossible to know.

The woman sounds concerned. "Naturally, Dr. Martin won't be her doctor of record there."

"I understand. Of course. The travel was unexpected. A family issue. Thank you for all you did for her."

I hang up, running in a dead sprint for my bedroom. I have no time to pack properly. I slide everything from my bathroom counter into a duffel bag, along with a pile of random clothes.

I call Devin. "I need a flight to Denver, Colorado, as soon as you can make one. Any class. Any airline. Any price. I'm about to get in an Uber. I'll head toward La Guardia but let me know if we should divert to JFK."

"Is this about Lucy?"

"She went into labor, and the nurses called her doctor here."

"That's great news! I'll get right on it."

Is it great news? I remember her standing in my office the first day, distraught that I was willing to miss the birth of my baby.

She was so sure. She was always so sure.

I've screwed up.

What's an apartment without your family in it?

What's a job if you hate it?

As I lock the front door, I say to it, "I'm never coming back here."

Now I have to find a way to make it true.

## 37

## LUCY

This baby is never coming.

It's been twelve hours.

The nurses aren't concerned yet, patting my knees and giving me patronizing lines like, "Babies come when they're ready."

*I'm* ready.

Mom's doctor has checked on me twice, glad to introduce himself before the big moment. "I delivered you, you know!" he says with a wink.

I'm so tired, but I can't sleep anymore. I'm not allowed to eat in case they need to intervene with a c-section. The waves of contractions don't hurt exactly, but I'm weary of feeling them. If one more person takes my blood pressure, I'm going to lose my mind!

I need a break from my hovering parents, so I insist they go check on Matilda. I ask Mom if I can borrow her phone while they're gone. I haven't gotten a new one yet.

When I'm finally alone in the room for ten seconds, I look up Pickle Media and call.

But I'm too late. I've forgotten we're two hours ahead of them and five o'clock here is seven there.

Why didn't I do it sooner?

But I know. I was worried I would be embarrassed in front of Mom and Dad. That Court wouldn't take my call. That Devin would sound sympathetic and sad for me.

Why didn't I memorize his cell phone? I try to recall the digits, but I've never dialed them, only used the contact list. I don't know them.

It's Friday. I won't get another chance to call him until Monday.

I curl up on my side around the roiling pressure in my belly. Sometime today or during the night, I'm going to become a mom.

A single mom.

Court feels a lifetime away.

I shouldn't have gone.

I made the wrong choice.

He was more important than Matilda. I could have taken her to the spa. Maybe Kaliyah could have held onto her for a while.

Why didn't I think of that before?

Then I sit up. Kaliyah. When he made the appointment, he called from his phone. They would have the number.

I quickly look up Wenova Wellness Spa and dial.

"This is Kristan."

"Is Kaliyah there?"

"She's off today. Can I help you?"

"I need the phone number off my account. I went there for a pedicure two weeks ago."

"Oh?" She sounds skeptical.

"My name is Lucy. Lucy Brown."

She taps.

"I don't have a Lucy Brown."

Right. He'd used his last name. "I meant Lucy Armstrong. What is the number for Lucy Armstrong?"

There's no tapping this time. "I'm sorry, we don't give out customer information."

"But it's my information!"

The silence continues.

Then Kristan hangs up!

The tears start again. Why couldn't I get Kaliyah? She knows I'm legit.

Maybe it doesn't matter. My situation with Court might not be fixable. I left him. I didn't even tell him where I'd gone. I didn't take the phone so he could call me.

My face burns hot. I want to throw up.

How can the best day of my life also be my worst?

I cry until I hiccup, then cry until I can't see the room anymore.

The nurse comes to check on me, taking my vitals. "Feeling okay?"

"Tired."

"It's been a long day. You want me to dim the lights while your parents are away? Maybe you can get some sleep?"

I nod, and she does. Then the room is quiet again.

It's just me and Julian. I wonder what he's thinking. His world is suddenly volatile, too, the peaceful utopia suddenly squeezing him from all sides.

I'm so uncomfortable. I roll to the opposite side, away from the door, and look out the slice of window visible below the blinds. It's dark outside. I've been here all day.

I hiccup-cry a little longer, but my mouth is so dry, it becomes yet another misery. I reach out for the cup of ice chips the nurse left behind, but they're out of range of my fingers.

I sense the door opening behind me, then a male voice. "Let me get that."

It must be a male nurse who's come on shift. He sounds like... Court.

I swipe at my bleary, swollen eyes. Maybe I'm wishing too hard. Delirious.

There's a figure there in the low light. Tall. Broad. But that hair is all wrong. Court never looks like he's been shocked by a light socket.

He picks up the cup and hands it to me.

I stare at him, unsure. This nurse isn't wearing scrubs.

He speaks again. "I'm guessing by the size of your belly that he's still in there."

It *is* Court!

I'm so shocked, I drop the cup on the bed. Ice spills everywhere. "How are you here?"

"Airplane. Had to bribe a college student to give me his seat." He sits on the edge of the bed. "Are you in pain?"

"No. I have an epidural. How did you know where to come?"

He bends over to pick up ice from the sheets. "Your Warwick doctor called me and told me where you were."

"This morning?"

"About ten hours ago."

"And you… came?"

He palms the dirty ice chips and straightens the cup, which is partially full. "I did."

I shove an ice chip in my mouth while he takes the fallen ones to the sink.

He's here!

But what does it mean?

I feel the need to clear up everything.

"I didn't know about the blood test," I say around the ice. "But I should have looked it up. I should have been prepared. I should have emailed you before I went to New York. I should have told you back when I found out in February. I—"

"Hey." He sits back down and brushes my hair from my face. "Let's move forward. Okay? Let's solve each problem as it comes, one at a time."

I nod. "Okay."

He leans down and kisses my forehead. At first, he smells like an airplane, and the city. Then I catch the scent of him. The beard oil. The citrus bath wash.

"What can I do for you?" he asks.

"Just be here."

He grips my hand. "I'm not going anywhere. Did you call your parents to come get you?"

"No. April and Summer did."

"But you made up with them?"

"They drove me and Matilda home."

He brings my hand to his lips. "You're staying with them?"

"We put my old nursery back together. Matilda is happy in the yard."

He kisses my knuckles. "Where do they live?"

"About a half hour between here and Boulder."

"My family lives in Boulder."

They do? "That's not far. Have you told them?"

"I called them when I landed. They're waiting for me to tell them it's okay to come."

I hesitate. "But we haven't done the test yet."

"We don't have to do the test."

Tears prick my eyes. We don't? "I'd like if we did."

"Then we will."

"Can he be Julian Armstrong?"

He kisses my hand again. "Yes, he can."

The pressure in my belly increases, and I find I can't lie on my side any longer. "Can you help me sit up?"

We work together to shift my position.

"Where are your parents?" he asks.

"I sent them away to check on Matilda. They'll be back in an hour."

"Do you want me to be here to meet them? I'm happy to do whatever you want."

"Yes. In fact, I'll text Dad so they know you're here."

I pick up Mom's phone, but then I'm hit with a contraction so big that I drop it.

Court lunges to catch it before it hits the floor.

Something weird is happening between my legs. I scrunch down. "Call the nurse, Court! Call the nurse!"

He fumbles with the remote for the hospital bed and slams the button.

"Where is she? Where is she?" Panic edges my voice.

"Should I turn on the light?"

I grip his arm in a vise. "Don't leave me!"

"Should I look?"

He flips the light on Mom's phone.

We lift my gown.

"That looks like a head to me," Court says. "Should I go get someone?"

I grab his arm. "Don't you dare leave me!"

The nurse enters, and the overhead light comes on. She takes one look down below and starts texting. "Let me page the doctor. You're doing great, Lucy!"

HOW CAN SHE BE SO CALM?

Then there's activity everywhere. Two more people come in, then a man with a plastic baby bed.

Then Dr. Fresno is back. "I hear we're having a baby!" He snaps on gloves and situates himself at the end of the bed. "Time to push, Lucy."

It's a blur then. The lights. The voices. The crowd of people. Mom and Dad return. They circle around.

The pressure is intense, coming and going, but coming back again so fast, I can barely catch a breath. I grip Court's hand. He smooths my hair.

Then the sensation is gone. Totally gone.

Everyone's quiet for a moment.

Then a cry.

A beautiful, piercing cry!

"It's a boy!" Dr. Fresno says.

The room comes back into focus. Mom hugs Dad.

Dr. Fresno lifts the baby, pink and covered partially in white, the cord hanging from his belly.

Court stays by my side, holding my hand. "It's Julian." He kisses my head.

Then the baby is on my chest. A bracelet is snapped to his wrist and ankle. Dr. Fresno listens to him with a stethoscope.

"Is he okay?" I ask, barely registering that it's all over, that he's here.

"He's perfect," Dr. Fresno says.

The nurse shifts the baby to lie on my skin and covers us both in a blanket.

The room empties.

"We'll give you two a moment," Mom says.

I don't know if she met Court. I don't know anything except there's this heavy, warm baby on my body, and Court is leaning over us both.

Nothing else matters.

Not a single other thing.

# 38

## COURT

I got here.

I made it.

He's born.

We sit there awhile, cuddled together at the top of Lucy's hospital bed.

Then people filter in again. It's time to clean the baby, they say, get him checked out.

The nurse takes the baby and swaddles him in a blanket.

Lucy's parents go to watch. We haven't officially met yet, but they seem to understand who I am.

Lucy gets cleaned up. I stay close to her face, my head pressed to hers. "You okay?" I whisper.

"More than okay," she says.

Finally, we're alone again.

"Can you get me some water?" she asks.

I head to the sink to fill a cup. I spot a roll of white gauze. I pick it up. There's something I have to do. It should be today.

I twist a strip of the narrow gauze and tie it around the end of my finger. I tuck it in on itself and pull it off, then continue wrapping more gauze around the circle until it's sturdy. I palm it as I return to her.

I pass her the water. She sips it. Sounds filter in from elsewhere in the hospital.

Any minute, her parents will return. The baby will return. The next stage will begin.

I take her hand and slide the gauze ring onto her left hand.

"What's this?" Her head tilts.

"Lucy, let's not waste any more time on the wrong path. Let's choose each other. Choose this family. Together. Will you marry me?"

She looks up at me, tears spilling down her face. "Okay," she says. "I choose you. You and Julian."

"And Matilda."

She laughs. "And Matilda."

"And her goat baby."

She laughs harder and presses on her belly. "And her baby."

I pull her into my embrace. We hold onto each other like survivors of a storm.

It feels right having her in my arms again. Like family. Like home. I have no idea what the future looks like. Where it will be. How we will shape it.

But I know it will be with her.

The door opens.

"Baby is back!" the nurse says, pushing the rolling bassinet next to the bed. Lucy's parents follow, videoing everything with their phones.

I help Lucy sit up. She takes the baby. So many photos are taken. I remember to take some, too.

Then he's passed to me. I don't know where to put my hands or my elbows, but the nurse arranges my arms.

He rests against my chest, nothing but a tight blanket, a hat, and a tiny face. His lips push together, and his eyebrows shift. I think he's going to cry, but then he relaxes again. It must be hard, having your entire world change.

I know how he feels.

I don't know how long I stand there, staring at him, but eventually, I look up. Everyone is watching me.

My first urge is to tell them to knock it off, to force their attention away.

But I don't. I take a deep breath and simply say, "I'm Court. I had to fly in from New York to make it. Nice to meet you."

Lucy reaches up to squeeze my arm. I sit close to her on the bed, and we hold the baby between us.

I'm not sure where we're going, but I know that wherever it is, we're doing it together.

By the time we leave the hospital, I'm an expert at making baby burritos and predicting when it's time for a new diaper or nursing.

At Lucy's parents' house, I sleep in Lucy's old room while she stays on the bed in the nursery for the first few nights, then we start taking turns.

Uncle Sherman calls about a week in to check on me. I shift Julian to the crook of my arm to take the call. Lucy is sleeping, and her parents are picking up groceries.

"How is fatherhood?" Sherman asks.

"Tiring."

"I remember. Did it three times." He hesitates. "Did you do the paternity test?"

"We did. All is in order."

"Was she upset that you asked for it?"

"I didn't. She wanted it. Wanted everything square."

"Good. Good."

I figure he wants to know if I'm coming back. "So, about Pickle Media," I say.

"I've got it covered. I've taken over your office. I'm handling the merch transition plus the yokels who think having the staff do a limbo competition at a company luau is going to fix morale."

"Yeah. Maybe they aren't the right fit."

"I'll take care of it. You just be a dad, and we'll figure things out when you're ready."

"And if I'm never ready?"

He laughs. "I guess I'll be writing a recommendation letter to the local 7-Eleven."

"I might be under-qualified to manage a convenience store, based on my human resources record."

"Now, now. Sometimes it's the system, not the leader. We'll take a good, hard look. You need anything here? Someone to check on your apartment?"

"My housekeeper is holding down the fort." I don't say that I already know I'm not going back.

"All right, then. You let us know if that new Pickle needs anything."

"He's an Armstrong."

Another gruff laugh. "Every Pickle's a Pickle."

Another week passes. Lucy seems more or less recovered, and we no longer look like zombies walking around the house. I rent an Airbnb a couple of blocks away, and we move there. We can't bring Matilda, but it's a quick stroller walk to check on her.

Matilda seems to understand that Lucy has had her baby, and, while she's skittish about Lucy herself, she likes the baby a lot. The moment we push the stroller into the backyard, she jumps and bleats. Then slowly and carefully, she sneaks close to the stroller to nudge the baby's foot.

Her goat belly is swelling, and I have about four months to figure everything out so the whole family can be reunited. I'll get it done. I have ideas.

When Julian is three weeks old, my parents come to visit.

I've been sending pictures and waiting until the time seems right, but they're eager to meet their first grandchild. When Lucy feels ready to be introduced, they make the quick drive to our rented house.

Mom comes in, her eyes on the baby, but she does the right thing and greets Lucy first. Only once everyone has been introduced do we relinquish Julian.

They order food and dote on the baby. Dad takes me aside and asks what the heck kind of ring Lucy is wearing?

"We haven't had time to go ring shopping. Lucy isn't fancy."

He nods. "I'd fix that."

"Did you check on that other matter for me?"

"I did. If it's out of your reach, Axel and I can help." He opens the bag of baby things they brought and passes me a sheaf of papers.

The number is high. I'll have to sell everything I own. Ferrari included.

Dumb thing doesn't have a proper back row for a car seat anyway.

Mom calls out to us. "Ronan, bring me that rattle that belonged to Court. I want a picture of Julian with it."

Dad digs through the bag and pulls out a toy with the head of Mickey Mouse on a stick.

"That'll give him nightmares," I say.

"Oh, hush," Mom says, reaching for it. "You loved it." She shakes it at Julian. "Lookie, sweet boy. It's Dada's rattle."

"I better take pictures," Dad says. "Why don't you go make a call before the close of business?"

Lucy looks up at me as I escape to the bedroom, but she stays with my parents and Julian.

I dial the number of the holding company on the page. The property isn't currently for sale, but I'm ready to play "Let's Make a Deal."

It's wild to be without the baby.

I wave at Mom and Dad as Court backs down the driveway in the SUV he bought when we moved to the Airbnb house.

Then I frantically roll down the window.

"Don't forget the bag balm! He's got a spot of diaper rash on his right side!"

"We won't!" Mom calls. She lifts Julian's hand to make him wave.

I roll up the window, then roll it down again. "There's two extra bags of breast milk in your freezer! Thaw them in hot water, not the microwave!"

"We've got it!" Dad calls.

Court pauses at the curb.

I look at him. "Are we going?"

"I'm giving you a second to see if you think of anything else."

"Oh, don't be silly. It's only a couple of hours." I wave at the steering wheel. "Let's go."

But as soon as Court lifts his foot from the brake, I hang out the window again. "His favorite song right now is *Look What You Made Me Do*. Play that if he's fussy."

Mom waves her hand dismissively, as if there's no way she's playing that song.

Court moves forward.

I roll up the window. "Did I remember everything?"

"I'm sure you did."

I set my phone in the lap of my blue cotton dress. I reclaimed all my clothes from the yurt a couple of weeks ago. "I can always text them anything I forgot."

"Exactly."

Court had all the baby things shipped from his apartment. Maggie is slowly packing everything small in advance of the team, who will eventually move all the furniture when he's ready for it.

He says he's never going back there. His home is here.

So far, so good. We're learning how to care for Julian together. Like he said in the hospital, we take each challenge one at a time. We almost never talk of the distant future, other than a vague notion that we'll know when it's time to have a wedding.

We head for the family-owned jewelry store to get a proper engagement ring, even though I told him I don't need one.

"Remember, I don't want any diamonds," I say. "Too much conflict. Too many bad apples in mining."

"Got it. But the fair-trade gold is okay?"

I nod. "Yes."

"What if we use estate gems from old family jewelry?"

"I guess that would be okay. We're not taking part in a trade with despicable practices."

Court nods, and I let out a slow breath of relief. He says I'm like an onion, and he's constantly revealing an additional layer of how I want the world to be, and what I won't be a part of. It's my choice. I don't force my beliefs on anyone, not even him.

Which can be evidenced by how many times my dad springs him from the house to get barbecue. I don't even mind the leftovers in the fridge, not that Court leaves any. The man loves his meat, and that's okay.

We pull up to the small store that specializes in ethically sourced gems and metals. Court takes my hand. As we enter the showroom with its lighted glass cabinets, I can't help but feel excited. "I'm in a Valentine's Day commercial," I tell Court.

He smiles as a young woman in a pink dress comes forward. "You must be Court."

"I am." He passes her a roll of velvet. The family jewels, I'm guessing.

"I'm Vicky, one of the designers here. You're Lucy?"

"Yes. And I like things simple."

"I understand completely," Vicky says. "Let's look at the family gems and see if we can come up with something you'll love." She unrolls the velvet.

Inside, clear plastic pockets each hold a gem, some large, some small. A couple of them are attached to their original settings. A single earring. A pendant.

"I see we have a couple of rubies, an emerald, sapphires, and several diamonds."

"Lucy doesn't like diamonds," Court says.

But they're so sparkly. "How old are these?" I ask.

"Some of them over a hundred years," he says. "My great-great-grandfather gave these earrings to my great-great grandmother, but then my great-grandfather accidentally grabbed one straight out of her ear and threw it into the Grand Canyon. Only one survived. But she kept it. It was his first gift to her."

"So much history." I run my fingers over the gems. "No one who mined or cut these is alive anymore."

Vicky nods. "Only their work remains."

It does seem a shame all this beauty is lost to the world. But it isn't practical for me.

"I like to work with my hands. I can't really have a big stone."

"Let me show you something I made before," Vicky says. She unlocks the next cabinet over and pulls out a black velvet display. She pulls a set of rings out and passes a wedding band to me.

"So, this solo band is lovely all on its own," she says. "It has two inlaid stones on each side of the swirl."

I examine it. It's beautiful, braided gold with four stones and a lovely loop in the middle.

"But then, on special occasions, the larger stone ring fits right inside." Vicky snaps an engagement ring with a ridiculously large diamond into the band.

It's breathtaking. "Court," I breathe. "I've never seen anything so pretty."

"You can have that one if you want it," Court says. "We don't have to use the family stones."

"Could we do it with your family's jewels? And maybe more of a 'v' shape than swirl?"

"That sounds lovely," Vicky says. "Do you have a preference on which of these gems to use?"

"I wouldn't know," I say. "I leave that up to you as long as you use these."

"All right," Vicky says. "Let us catalog them before we take them to be used. I'll be right back."

Court and I wait by the counter. "You sure?" he asks.

I feel lightheaded with giddiness. "So, we're doing this? Getting married?" I lean in. "You haven't even had sex with me since before Julian was born."

He bends close to my ear. "And hasn't enough time passed for that?"

I meet his gaze. "It has."

"And our house is empty?"

I grin. "It is."

Vicky returns with a photograph of the gems and forms for Court to sign.

"Give us a few weeks," she says. "I'll contact you with some sketches."

Court and I practically run back to the car.

"Are we headed for a booty call?" I ask.

"Yes," he says. "But I have another stop first."

"Condoms?"

He laughs. "Definitely need those. But something else."

As we head out of the Denver suburb I grew up in, I

recognize the highway we're traveling. "Why are we going this way?" My belly quivers. It's how we used to go to Grandma BeeBee's.

"We should take a look," Court says.

"I might get upset."

He reaches over to take my hand. "Let's face it together."

As we crest the last hill before you can see her farm, I have to squeeze my eyes shut. I need to prepare myself. It could be a liquor store. Or God help me, a butcher shop.

I let out a long, slow breath. I picture the farm in its best days, in the summer, the front rail heavy with flow-ered vines, the berry bushes bursting with fruit. The barn doors would be thrown open where Grandpa would endlessly work on his latest project car, a classic BMW or maybe an old Mustang. He especially loved 1950s Ford trucks.

"I have something for you," Court says. He tugs my hand from where I'm gripping my skirt and places something papery in my palm.

I open my eyes, careful to avoid looking up or out the window.

"What's this?"

"Take a peek."

I slide my finger under the flap. Inside is a folded sheaf of pages.

And a key.

The key is new and shiny. I turn to Court. "What's this the key to?"

He points out the front window. "They changed the locks when it first sold."

I hold his gaze for a moment. "What are you saying?"

"I'm saying the development deal from five years ago fell through when the holding company filed for bankruptcy. BeeBee's farm went into foreclosure and got hung up for two more years. A year ago, it sold to another developer, who hasn't yet decided what to do with the property."

My entire body flashes hot, then cold.

Is it true?

I look up.

And it's there.

It looks terrible. Paint peeling, porch listing, weeds overtaking everything.

But it's there.

"Court! Court!" I can't think of anything else to say. "Court!"

"It's yours, Lucy. We're not married yet, so it's just yours. If you get rid of me some time in the future, it will still be yours, since it will predate our wedding."

I lean over and kiss him. "I can't believe it!"

I wrestle with the door. Finally, it opens, and I race across the cracked drive to the overgrown yard.

I stop at the collapsing porch and take off around the house to the back door. This side has only a concrete step.

I try the lock, and the key works back here. I pause for a moment, turning to look over the barn and yard that was once my most familiar view.

It's still here!

The back door opens with a squeal of rusty hinges. The kitchen has the same wood cabinets and linoleum floor. It's dirty and filled with spiderwebs, but it's the same as I remember it.

I dash to the empty dining room. The curtains are on the window! I brush them with my hand, sending a flutter of patterned light on the walls from the lace.

I can almost *feel* Grandma BeeBee here.

Next is the living room with the old stone fireplace. The furniture has been cleared out, but the old oval rug made of tied rags sits in front of it.

I drop to my knees on it. If I don't pay too close attention to the dust, I can almost imagine that their two matching recliners are behind me. BeeBee is doing a cross stitch, and Grandpa is squinting at his phone and wishing for a newspaper.

The thought makes me smile, and I hold onto the moment as long as possible.

Then I'm up again and walking down the hall. The small front bedroom. The hall bathroom. The funny cutout in the wall with a shelf above the old defunct landline jack. The middle bedroom. Then BeeBee's bedroom with its big sunny windows and attached bathroom.

It's all here.

A shuffle on the floor makes me turn around. Court stands in the door with a folded blanket and a picnic basket from Mom's pantry.

"Thought we could have an early dinner here before we head back."

I rush up to him and wrap my arms around his neck. He lowers the basket and lets me hold onto him, his lips in my hair.

"I love you," I say, and I'm surprised to find that I mean it. I'm not sure how love is supposed to grow or how long it's supposed to take, but I feel it.

"I love you too, Lucy."

I pull back. "Is it too fast?"

His expression is serious. Not the salty kind, the one I first knew. But earnest. "I think maybe it will only grow stronger from here."

I take the blanket from him. "Let's eat in the living room. The old rug is there. It will give us extra padding."

"For dinner?" he asks.

"No," I say. "For breaking in my new house."

He sets the basket on the floor. "In that case, we're walking way too slow."

He picks me up and throws me over his shoulder.

I let out a squeal. It feels amazing, my body so close to his, only a normal belly between us.

When he sets me down in front of the fireplace, he does it slowly, carefully, until my feet are back on the ground.

Then he kisses me and undresses me, and we spread the blanket and remind ourselves of how we got in this predicament in the first place. Kisses. Touches. His mouth everywhere on my body.

Then he jumps up and runs, naked, back to the basket, where he's stashed the condoms.

When we're bundled up in the blanket as the sky

gets dark, I tell him, "I think we're going to be very happy here. I can teach Julian how to milk Matilda. Where to spot bearberries." I poke his chest. "Of course, we'll have to figure out how to support ourselves."

"We will." Court draws me close. "I think we're going to need more goats."

# EPILOGUE: LUCY

*Five months later.*

Spring is a beautiful season at BeeBee's farm. I peer out the window as Mom sticks another pin in my veil. It was hers originally, but we found a TikTok video about how to bleach the yellowing out of it to use it again.

Everything I wear is old, other than my wedding ring. We refashioned BeeBee's gown, which Dad found stored in the trunks he'd put in storage after selling the farm.

I learned he kicked in quite a bit of money to help Court buy it for me. It's a gift from two of my best three men.

The third one lies on his back on a blanket, shaking the Mickey Mouse rattle he's finally figured out how to grasp. He's my something blue in a smart baby suit.

"You ready?" Mom asks. "I hear the music starting."

I nod.

I touch the old pine furniture that Court carved with his grandfather as I walk through the room. Court has made a new piece for the set, a bookcase, and in it, I've placed all of BeeBee's cookbooks and sewing manuals that were stored in trunks.

His new wood shop is fully operational in Grandpa's work barn, and the orders are slowly trickling in. Between that and my yoga classes, we've been getting by. It helps that the house is paid for.

Matilda is due any day, and once we're getting goat cheese money again, I'll increase the size of our herd to get a hobby farm going.

My dream is alive.

Court's dream is alive.

And today, we bring them together.

Dad comes in the door. "Don't you look beautiful," he says.

"Thank you, Daddy."

"I'll go on ahead," Mom says.

"See you in the backyard," I tell her.

I pick up Julian. It might have been fun to wait until he could walk down the aisle himself, but about a month ago, Court and I felt the moment come. "Let's get married when the irises bloom," I told him. "That's the first sign of spring."

And we did. One thing neglect can never take away are the bulbs in the ground, and BeeBee's irises came up sure as sunrise in late February with sticks of green.

We set the wedding for mid March, and as I step out onto the back porch, I know no florist could make a prettier pathway than the snow-white blooms lining her walkway, lines of chairs on either side.

Everyone stands, and Julian makes a great shout as everyone moves. Laughter titters through the group.

Dad squeezes my arm, and we begin our walk up to the front, Court's sister Nadia singing with their Grammy off to the side. They both have lovely voices.

Court's brothers Rhett and Axel stand on the right side of the archway my grandfather built decades ago, covered in vines just now leafing out.

April and Summer wait on the other side of the arch, having walked up the aisle ahead of me.

Then Court steps to the center to wait for me, and his shining eyes are all I can focus on. When we get to the front, he kisses Julian's head, then I pass the baby to my father for my parents to hold.

The minister moves behind us and begins the traditional ceremony. "We come together today to join in marriage Lucy Brown and Court Armstrong."

I hear Julian babbling as we say our vows. Court's grip on my hand is sure and firm. When I say, "I do," his smile is so big, it's hard to believe he was ever salty at all.

"You may kiss the bride," the minister says.

When his lips meet mine, there is a great cheer. I smile against Court's mouth. "We did it," I tell him.

"We did."

I take his hand and am about to accept the baby from my mother when I hear an unexpected sound.

Matilda?

I turn to look through the arch at the corner of the fenced yard attached to the barn.

Matilda is climbing the wood slats, bleating through the gaps.

"You think she's happy for us?" Court asks.

"Maybe." I turn to take a step closer.

Matilda's bleats grow in intensity. Then I can't see her.

"Matilda?" I rush to the fence, grasping handfuls of the long skirt to keep it out of my way.

She's lying on her side, panting. Her belly moves in and out. She bleats again.

"She's in labor!" I cry, kicking off my satin pumps and climbing the low fence. "Baby girl!"

I kneel next to her. "Get some towels and water! We're having another baby!"

Everyone scurries to help. Once we have her settled, old farmer friends of BeeBee offer to watch over her so we can cut the cake.

I look down at my dirty dress. "I guess this is about the way it's going to be," I tell Court. The knees of his tux are as grimy as mine.

He takes my hand. "I wouldn't have it any other way."

Want to read about that crazy night on New Year's Eve when Lucy and Court had their life-changing 90-minute one-night stand?

Visit jjknight.com/getepilogue to sign up for it (plus bonus material to her other comedies!)

Otherwise, welcome to the Pickleverse! Go see all the books on retailers or at JJKnight.com.

## CHARACTERS WITH THEIR OWN BOOKS

- **Court's older brother Rhett** gets himself in a real pickle when the assistant he fired shows up on the company cruise. Their big argument on a private island is so heated they end missing the boat back and have to weather a storm in complete solitude on the deserted island in Juicy Pickle.
- **Court's younger brother Axel** meets his match on a hiking trail in a situation only a rom com could get away with in Tasty Pickle.
- **Uncle Sherman** raised a whole brood of sons. Read their hilarious adventures in romance in the original Pickle trilogy: Big Pickle, Hot Pickle, and Spicy Pickle.

# BOOKS BY JJ KNIGHT

### *Romantic Comedies*

Big Pickle ~ Hot Pickle ~ Spicy Pickle

Tasty Mango ~ Tasty Pickle ~ Tasty Cherry

Royal Pickle ~ Royal Rebel ~ Royal Escape

Juicy Pickle ~ Salty Pickle

Second Chance Santa

The Wedding Confession

The Wedding Shake-up

Not Exactly a Small-Town Romance

Single Dad on Top ~ The Accidental Harem

### *MMA Fighters*

Uncaged Love ~ Fight for Her ~ Reckless Attraction

Get emails or texts from JJ about her new releases:

JJKnight.com/news

# ABOUT JJ KNIGHT

 JJ Knight is one of the pen names of six-time *USA Today* bestselling author Deanna Roy. She lives in Austin, Texas, with her family.

Visit her at jjknight.com.